THE CAPTAIN AND THE LADY

"So you are your father's hostess," the captain said mockingly. "Does he try to model you in his fashion? Yes, I can see that he tries. But you have warmth in you, under that ice."

Diana stiffened, and drew away from him. "Sir, you are impertinent!"

"It is my nature," his reckless voice murmured in her ear. "What did they do to you, Lady Diana? When your mother died, did all warmth die with her?"

She bit her lip, aware of a desire to slap him. He only laughed softly as if he understood that, too.

"I have the impression, my lady, that you have never been loved," he whispered, his arms closing about her. *"You should be, you know."*

The
Heart Awakens

A Regency Romance

Janette Radcliffe

A DELL BOOK

Published by
Dell Publishing Co., Inc.
1 Dag Hammarskjold Plaza
New York, New York 10017

Dell ® TM 681510, Dell Publishing Co., Inc.

ISBN: 0-440-13525-7

Printed in the United States of America

First printing—October 1977

Chapter 1

"Beautiful Diana, goddess of the moon," the admirer murmured in Diana's ear as they slowly circled the room. "So chaste, so remote—" They paused at the card table, and she pretended to study the play, thinking she really must get away from this gentleman. He was just drunk enough to be annoying.

She caught the eye of Sir Geoffrey Loring, and he came over to her at once. The admirer melted away. Sir Geoffrey was Lady Diana Somerville's fiancé and his possessiveness toward her was well known. Moreover, his standing was high in the diplomatic corps, and it did not pay to cross him.

Diana smiled gratefully at Sir Geoffrey as he took her arm and continued the promenade of the room. "Was that boor bothering you?" he growled.

"He was in his cups," she said mildly. She knew better than to complain, for her fiancé's vile temper was easily aroused. "He is pleasant enough, though."

Sir Geoffrey frowned back at the man rapidly stumbling through the spectators at the gaming table. He seemed about to go after the fellow, but Diana pressed his arm to regain his attention.

"Did you manage to have your talk with the prince?" she asked in a lower tone.

"No, dammit— Beg pardon. Coy as a young damsel about talking politics," Sir Geoffrey complained. "These Russian princes are as temperamental as the Frenchies. Wouldn't be surprised if he is playing us against each other."

So Geoffrey had not had his way this evening; he would be difficult to soothe. Lady Diana suppressed a great sigh. She was accomplished in her role of smoother of ruffled feathers since she had done it for her father, Lord Hubert Somerville, for many years. But lately, she had become oddly wearied of it.

Sometimes she wondered how it would be to have someone take care of her for a change, someone who loved her enough to want to make things smooth and comfortable. Someone who loved her . . . There she stopped.

Her mother had died when she was ten. The memory was dim of that cool blonde beauty, the gentleness of her white hands, the rare occasions when her mother had come to tuck her into bed, to bend and kiss her forehead. More often she had been left to the attentions of a nurse or governess, while her mother went off to grand affairs given by the diplomatic corps. She remembered her mother as a vision in blue and silver, or gold and drifting white, her smile strained and weary at times.

Since then, no one had loved Diana, and she had loved no one. Her father was cold and calculating, deeply involved in matters of state where his cool, analytical brain was an asset. Her brother, Thomas, was caught up in his own concerns, and six years her elder besides. At twenty, Diana was in her third London season, and her father was impatient to have the girl off his hands. Beauty, dressed properly and bejeweled, was expensive.

Several men had offered for her, in spite of the coolness which had earned her the reputation of "Lady Iceberg." Just two months ago, her father had accepted Sir Geoffrey's offer, and told Diana she was fortunate to receive it. Sir Geoffrey was bound to have a fine career as a diplomat, had a title in his own right, and was an undeniably attractive man.

If only Diana could feel his attraction! She noted the admiring looks that followed them both. But somehow she hated to feel Sir Geoffrey's arm about her; she avoided his kisses. Something in her felt deeply repelled by him. Perhaps it was the sight one day of him beating his servant for some small offense. Perhaps it was his cold analysis of people, followed by an effusive courtesy toward them that smoothly covered his real feelings. She had the notion sometimes that he did not even like her, that he craved only her body, her position. She was a suitable match.

Was there nothing else in the world but a "proper" marriage? Did no one marry for love anymore? In society, perhaps love was no longer in fashion, she thought, and her mouth curved in bitterness.

Sir Geoffrey spotted his prey, Prince Alexei Troubetzkoy, and steered her toward the man. The Russian diplomat bowed to them, his flashing green eyes met Diana's, and she felt a thrill go through her. She liked the devilish laughter in his eyes. His wife, Nadia, was near him, and drifted toward them at his gesture. Nadia was tall and slim, her great dark eyes passionate.

They stood and talked idly. Sir Geoffrey grew expansive, but the prince persisted in keeping the talk to trivialities.

"You are the talk of the ballroom, Lady Diana," he said. "My wife admires your gown greatly. Is the name of your dressmaker a dark secret?"

They all gazed at Diana in the stunning blue-green gown with an underdress of taffeta and an overskirt of gauze that rippled like a sea wave, crested with delicate white lace.

"You are very kind, Your Highness," she replied, and smiled at Nadia. "I go to one of the excellent French ladies in the Strand, Madame Berthe. She seems to understand what I like, and is making several new gowns for our trip to America."

"Ah, you go to America," Nadia murmured longingly. "How marvelous! You must look forward to this journey, yes? And with your fiancé and your father? You will be married soon?"

"Not until we return," said Diana firmly. She

felt a little sick when she thought of that marriage. Could they not put it off longer—forever?

The prince glanced down at his wife just then, and Diana caught the tender understanding in his look, saw the slight pressure of his fingers on her gloved arm. "You shall travel with me to the Mediterranean, my darling, when I go," he said gently. "Nadia enjoys seeing new places very much," he explained to the others with a slight laugh.

And he enjoyed giving her pleasure, thought Diana. A moment later he asked Diana to join in the cotillion that was forming, and she put her hand on his green and gold-clad arm. Sir Geoffrey had to offer for Nadia, and followed them crossly. He had not been able to lure the prince into the serious conversation he had wished.

"Have you been married long?" asked Diana abruptly. The prince gazed down at her in surprise. She did not usually make such personal remarks.

"Five years, my lady. My Nadia and I are blessed with two beautiful children."

"You are—fortunate," she said, thinking that he had spoken of his wife and children lovingly; his face had softened perceptibly.

"Not *fortunate*," he stressed with a smile. "My Nadia and I have been acquainted with each other since childhood. I watched her grow up, observed her beautiful nature, her—her sweetness and graciousness. As men admired her, she did not change to a spoiled beauty, as some do. She remained her unaffected self. We can laugh together, my Nadia and I. We enjoy the same things. That is what makes a marriage of such joy that one cannot explain it."

"I envy you," she murmured, then flushed, and changed the topic. The prince was looking too thoughtful.

After the dance, Sir Geoffrey disappeared into the card room, where the men were gaming for higher stakes. When he was upset, he gave vent to his ill humor by defeating warmer natures with his cold, detached playing, and he would remain there for hours sometimes. Diana looked about for her chaperone, and went to sit beside her.

Mrs. Smith-Crompton moved quickly to make room for her, anxiously eyeing the smooth face of her charge. A distant cousin, for some years widowed, Anne Smith-Crompton had been grateful for the task of caring for Diana and escorting her to parties and balls. But her continued employment depended on pleasing both Diana and Diana's strict father, and she was continually nervous about this.

"You are enjoying yourself, my dear?" she murmured.

Diana opened her fan of blue-green feathers, and wafted a breeze to her warm face. "Exceedingly," she said politely.

Mrs. Smith-Crompton was not fooled. She had seen Sir Geoffrey disappear into the card room. That young man would lose his lovely and wealthy fiancée if he did not show more affection for her. Yet—yet Lady Diana seemed to want none of his affection.

To the chaperone's relief, Madame Castel took a seat next to Diana. The society leader, a formidable woman with a sharp wit, was a favorite of Lady Diana's, and the girl's face brightened.

"You have made a conquest of the good prince," murmured Madame Castel. "What did you discuss so earnestly?"

"The elements of a happy marriage," smiled Diana. "He seems to have found them, do you not think so?"

The plump lady shrugged. "He is wealthy, his wife is beautiful, she has borne him an heir. Is that what you mean?"

Lady Diana smiled—a strange smile, thought Mrs. Smith-Crompton with growing unease. Her charge had been difficult since the grand occasion of the announcement of her engagement. She was restless, given to sitting in corners with an open book and not turning a page for an hour. Then she would start up, and go out to the stables, to ride a horse wildly for two hours across the open countryside.

And Lord Hubert Somerville had often been restless and upset of late. Of course, the recent troubles in the new United States—the colonies which had so stupidly revolted—seemed to be growing. Perhaps they had seen the error of their ways. Now it was 1812, and the years of independence might have made them see how foolish they were to withdraw from Great Britain. They might be willing to rejoin the mother country. Lord Hubert was going to America on a diplomatic mission, under guise of a trade mission. Sir Geoffrey and his fiancée would accompany him, and marry on their return in six months.

What would happen when the betrothed couple were so closely in touch for six months? They struck sparks from each other even now, in the course of a single evening, thought Mrs. Smith-Crompton. Sir Geoffrey did not handle her right, that was quite evident.

Madame Castel had turned the conversation to the latest *on-dits* about the Prince Regent, bending her head confidingly to Lady Diana's ear. The older woman was obviously amused at her own story, but Lady Diana scarcely smiled. Oh, dear, this was going to be a difficult evening, her chaperone thought.

Sir Peter Flanders came up then and bowed over Diana's hand. She smiled graciously at his request for a dance, made her apologies to Madame Castel, and departed with him. Presently her chaperone saw her laughing, and relaxed in great relief. The lad was charming; her charge would be all right.

Peter *was* amusing, Diana admitted to herself as they left the dance and he guided her toward some of his friends who stood about the lavish buffet tables. All were talking of the magnificent town house the Russian prince had rented for his stay in London.

The ballroom occupied the second floor of the

enormous four-storied mansion. From this splendid room, doors opened into a number of private rooms, most of which were presently occupied by cardplayers earnestly engaged in their games.

Diana gazed about the ballroom with its multi-tiered crystal chandeliers, its mirrored panels which covered one wall. She saw herself reflected in the mirrors, a girl with blonde curls floating to her shoulders, and misty gauze skirts swirling about her. Turning away abruptly from her reflection, she accepted a glass of wine, and gaily bantered with the elegant young men who hovered about her.

But Diana was bored. She wondered at herself. The first season in London had been so bright and amusing. The second had been considerably less enchanting, for she had had the unpleasant task of fighting off a number of ardent swains. This third season she had been fretful and restless, and had found herself preoccupied with the thought that she could not endure this kind of life for long. Yet the man she was to marry reveled in just such a life; for a diplomat such as Sir Geoffrey, this splendid ballroom was no more than the setting for political intrigue. For Diana it had become a dazzling prison.

A clock chimed midnight. It was quite proper for her to leave. Only where was Sir Geoffrey? He had promised to escort her home with her chaperone. The London streets were dangerous, stalked by gangs of rascals and Mohawks waiting to swoop down on the rich.

He must be deeply involved in his card game, or more likely in a political discussion, she thought. Perhaps he was in one of the small reception rooms. She looked about for Sir Peter Flanders, but he was devotedly bending down to listen to the bright chatter of one of the season's loveliest debutantes.

She set her chin. She would not remain a moment longer. She would find Sir Geoffrey. She left the ballroom and went to the first of several rooms.

She tapped, and opened the door to a cloud of cigar smoke. Five men were gathered about the card table. She smilingly apologized and closed the door again. The second room brought no luck, nor the third or the fourth. Where was Sir Geoffrey?

At the end of the hallway was another room she had not noticed. She hesitated, then tried the knob. It opened easily to her hand. She stepped inside a silent room. It seemed to be a study, darkened, the draperies drawn. Only a brace of candlesticks were alight on the study desk

She blinked. She could not believe— On a sofa near the desk Sir Geoffrey was sprawled, wearing only his undergarments! And on his brief white lawn trousers were borders of lace! She stared in amazement until a movement caught her eye.

She whirled about to see a tall man who stepped forward into the light. He was yanking on Sir Geoffrey's brilliant crimson jacket with its distinctive trim of gold braid. And he already wore the cream-colored trousers, the shining boots! A pile of discarded clothing near the couch told the story: he had discarded the uniform of a waiter.

She opened her mouth to scream. With incredible swiftness, the man darted forward, grabbed her, and clapped his huge hand over her mouth. With the other hand he shut the door softly behind her. She was trapped in the room with him.

She glared at him over the edge of his palm. He stared down at her. His hair was bronze-gold, but in form he resembled Sir Geoffrey, tall and broad-shouldered. His brilliant green eyes blazed down at her.

"Well, what have I here?" muttered the man in an unusual accent. He was not British, not French, she was sure of that. He slurred the words in a near drawl. She struggled in his grip. "A pretty captive, yes, indeed." He looked down at her slim body, its curves outlined in gauze. "Here's a pickle," he mused, as though to himself.

She struggled again, striking him with her fist. It hit a broad chest, so hard she thought she could break her hand against it.

The desk, she saw now, was covered with papers. Drawers had been hastily opened and emptied. It must be Prince Troubetzkoy's study. And this man had been rifling the drawers!

She glared at him, trying to hide her fear. He could kill her for seeing him here. And Sir Geoffrey—was he dead? She glanced toward her fiancé and flinched to see him lying helpless—in his undergarments!

"You know him?" demanded the hard voice in her ear.

She managed a nod.

"If you even squeak," he said calmly, "I'll kill him. Well, going to keep your mouth shut?"

He was a rude, vulgar man—a ruffian!

She wriggled in his grip, which only closed more tightly.

"No, no good," he said, and there was laughter in his voice. "I'm much tougher than you are, my girl!"

She glared her outrage.

"Going to be good?"

She finally nodded, and the grip over her mouth eased. He held her hatefully close, one arm clamped about her, the other hand over her mouth, slowly easing away.

"Who is the sprig?" he demanded.

She swallowed. "Sir—Geoffrey—Loring," she managed to say.

"What's he to you?"

"My—fiancé."

"Oh, indeed? And what is your name?" he mocked.

She would have screamed, but the green eyes were narrowed alertly. "I am Lady Diana Somerville."

"Somerville? Kin to Lord Hubert Somerville?"

She was surprised that he knew her father. This man must be a spy! But what accent did he have?

"My father," she said finally.

"Hm. Well, that's neither here nor there. Come

along, my dear." He clapped one hand over her wrist and drew her with him to the desk. Still holding her, he stuffed the papers into his shirt, then buttoned it securely again. The jacket was fastened over it.

"Now to get out of here—" His green eyes went to the windows. They were on the second floor, three floors from the ground. "No help for it. We must go out boldly," he murmured. "Well, my lady, you can help me. Give me your reticule."

Before she knew it, he had the little golden reticule from her wrist. "You would rob me also?" she asked spitefully. She had only a few golden coins with her.

He grinned at her and released her wrist, but kept watching her while he fumbled in the golden bag. "Ah, here it is. You ladies always carry some powder; I know from experience." He drew it out. Ridiculously, she wondered how he knew that ladies carried powder in their handbags. "Put some on my hair," he demanded.

"*What?*" Surely he could not be serious! He glared at her, and silently held out the little box of powder.

Her mouth tight with annoyance, she took the box. He bent his head, and she sifted powder over the bronze locks, crisp under her fingers. Impatiently he ran his fingers through his hair, scattering the powder about. Now, with his hair powdered like Sir Geoffrey's, he looked little like the golden-haired stranger of moments before.

"Enough," he said. He stuffed the box back into the reticule and put it on her wrist again. "Now, my lady, you'll get me to the front door and out."

"You are mad," she said quietly.

"All Americans are mad." He grinned at her.

Americans! So that was it. He was an American, and a very brazen one, too. Spying on a Russian prince in the middle of a ball!

"I will not protect you," she said, facing him, her chin up, her breathing coming hard. He might kill her for it. She had glimpsed the dagger strapped to the hard wrist under his crimson sleeve.

"Did I ask you to protect me?" He was chuckling softly. "Come along, my girl! I'll have a dance with you! You can waltz, can't you? I hear the music now—"

She hesitated. She waltzed rarely, and then only with her fiancé. It was not the thing to waltz with others, and many debutantes did not perform the daring dance at all. Yet she knew the steps. . . . "Yes, I can."

"I thought so. You move like a summer breeze," and his bold look went over her slim body again.

Why was she pleased at this compliment? She must be as mad as this demented spy. She glanced back uneasily at Sir Geoffrey, but he still lay limply on the sofa.

"Oh, he'll be out for a time. We had a bit of a dustup when he caught me rifling the desk," said the man with a chuckle and a glitter of green eyes.

"My clothes got ripped, so I decided to change with him. Fortunately, we're of a size. Fairly good fighter," he added with grave approval, but that laugh still quirked at the corner of his bold mouth.

He caught her wrist and drew her to the door with him. The waltz beckoned enticingly from the ballroom. He led her out the door and closed it firmly after him. He put his arm about her waist and bent his face to hers, so none could see his face. At the edge of the ballroom floor, he swept her into the waltz, holding her more tightly than any man had ever dared.

She felt the strangest mixture of feeling as he whirled her about, again and again, laughing down at her. His head was still bent to hide his face; all would recognize the crimson jacket and think she danced with her fiancé. Around and around, toward the ballroom door, she was whirled and spun until she was dizzy.

He spun her out the door, into the shadows. The bent head came closer, and for an instant she felt the man's bold mouth on hers. He held her tightly for a moment, then drew back and bowed deeply to her.

"Thank you, my lady— Farewell!" And he was gone, dashing into the deepest shadows. He drew a few curious looks, but all thought he was Sir Geoffrey.

Diana turned back into the ballroom, feeling queerly faint. It was the waltz, it had made her dizzy, dancing so fast, so very close to him. And the sudden release from fear . . .

But somehow she could not forget the warm, passionate touch of his mouth on hers, that bold, impudent kiss. It was the first time any man had dared to touch her so.

Chapter 2

Lady Diana returned to her chaperone and stood for a moment regaining her breath. Her breast rose and fell quickly. Her eyes glittered in the light from the chandeliers.

"I would like to leave, ma'am," she said breathlessly. "Do you see Sir Geoffrey anywhere?"

"I thought he was with you," said the good lady, puzzled. "Were you not waltzing with him?"

"I thought so at first," said Diana, opening and closing her fan rapidly. "But the man was a stranger! He swept me into the dance before I could do more than catch a glimpse of him."

An outcry interrupted their low conversation. Everyone in the ballroom turned toward a doorway where several men had gathered about an agitated figure. Diana bit her lips. She must not laugh. Geoffrey had wrapped a drapery about himself. Now, his hair on end, he was complaining loudly.

"Why, it is Sir Geoffrey!" exclaimed Mrs. Smith-Crompton. "Whatever in the world—"

Diana followed her chaperone slowly across the ballroom floor. Prince Alexei was questioning Geoffrey. The prince's aide had apparently dashed to the study, for he now returned and en-

gaged the prince in earnest discussion. There was
an air of great agitation about the men.

"What is it? What happened?" everyone was
asking.

Diana waited nearby, a still, tense figure.

Sir Geoffrey's voice rose. "A damned Yankee
spy!" he said. "Caught him in the very act of
searching the desk—"

Someone hushed him. Sir Peter Flanders approached Diana. "My lady, the prince would
speak with you." His troubled look brushed over
her. "You were dancing with the man, the impostor, were you not?"

"Impostor? What do you mean?" Diana moved
swiftly toward the prince. Sir Geoffrey seemed to
flinch from her, suddenly realizing the figure he
cut in the ridiculous drapery. She did not look at
him. She would not for the world reveal that she
had seen him unconscious and partially stripped.

Prince Troubetzkoy faced her gravely. "Lady
Diana, you were waltzing with a gentleman a few
moments ago. Did you know the man?"

"He was dressed in a coat very like Sir Geoffrey's," she answered. "Only at the door did I see
his face."

"From what direction did he come?" asked the
prince, eyeing her rather sternly.

She pointed. "That direction, Your Highness. I
had been searching for Sir Geoffrey, as I was
weary and wished to leave. This man appeared,
wearing Sir Geoffrey's clothes— I can scarcely be-

lieve I was so foolish, but I took him for Sir Geoffrey!"

"Ah, you did not see his face then?"

"No, his head was bent as we danced."

There was more murmuring and whispering. "He must have taken Sir Geoffrey's clothes and escaped with the papers," concluded the prince thoughtfully. "Then he was of a build—"

"He was an enormous man, my height or more," Geoffrey said in great agitation. "I do not know how he managed to struggle into my clothing. He knocked me out with a blow—"

Diana bit her lip, trying not to laugh. They would think her hysterical. She recalled the Yankee's description of the fight—"a bit of a dust-up"—and wanted to laugh aloud. Geoffrey would never admit it was a fair fight with a man his own size. No, his pride would not permit that.

"Well, I had best examine my desk, and see what is missing. Pray return to the dancing," said the prince. He smiled, but there was a hard gleam in his eyes.

Lady Diana turned to her chaperone. "Let us leave," she said in a low voice. "Sir Geoffrey cannot escort us home, but we will manage. I am most weary."

Mrs. Smith-Crompton hesitated. "I don't know what your father will say—"

"He will know little of it," said Diana impatiently. "And I do not mean to remain here all the night. Come!" And she swept the timid woman down the magnificent staircase to the ground floor, where a footman hurried to fetch their cloaks.

As Diana drew her blue velvet cloak about her shoulders, she was surprised to find herself shaking a little. It had all happened so quickly. And she must not be involved in a scandal. Nor would she have Geoffrey know—not for the world—that she had seen him in white lawn drawers trimmed with lace. Lace! And she pressed her white handkerchief to her mouth to keep back hysterical giggles.

The vanity of the man!

She left a message for her fiancé and called for her carriage. There was a little delay while they stood on the wide veranda of the town house, shivering in the night air. Finally her coachman, Justin, drove up with her closed carriage.

A gentleman Diana knew slightly was just coming from the house. He stepped forward to help her inside. She smiled and thanked him, and stepped up into the coach. She was just settling down and moving over to make room for her chaperone, when she made out the dark form opposite her.

A gleaming pistol shone on them, visible in the lights of the torches beyond the carriage. She caught the gleam also of eyes and of the face muffled in the stranger's dark cloak.

"Not a word, or I shoot," he whispered.

She sank into the seat, and pressed Mrs. Smith-Crompton's hand reassuringly.

The gentleman peered into the carriage. "My

lady, will you have my escort homeward? Your escort cannot accompany you, I warrant!" and he laughed good-naturedly.

Diana felt a hand on her arm, and the dark figure whispered in so light a tone the wind could have blown it away. "Tell him you need no one but your coachman!"

"Thank you, sir, I need no one but my coachman. He has been with me for years," Diana replied with a calmness that amazed her. Her hand gripped the shaking arm of her chaperone warningly.

The coachman called to his horses, and the carriage rolled over the cobblestones and out into the street. The man leaned back.

"You waltz beautifully, my lady," he said lightly, and she heard the laughter in his tone.

"Thank you, sir. I presume you mean to rob us and leave us dead?"

Mrs. Smith-Crompton gasped.

"No, no, I wish merely a ride upon my way," he said. "When I heard them call for Lady Somerville's carriage, I took my opportunity. You had been kind once, so I thought to take advantage—"

"Take advantage, indeed, sir! You are a thief and a spy!"

"Harsh words, my lady." His tone held a stern warning. Then it lightened. "How beautiful you looked this evening. The fashions seem somewhat extreme to my provincial eye, but the low cut becomes you mightily."

She flushed as she had not done in years, and

pressed her hand to her bosom. It *was* low cut, but that was the style, showing the rounded curve of her breasts.

"My sisters will be interested in the account I shall give them of this ball," he resumed, as though entertaining her with casual conversation. "They long to hear the latest *on-dits* of London. These wide bonnets, for instance, are they the style, my lady?"

She was determined to seem as calm as he. "Indeed, sir, the smaller bonnets are going out of fashion, and the wider the brim the more admired. My newest bonnet has some five inches of brim, and is trimmed with ribbons a yard long."

"Amazing," he murmured. "I should enjoy seeing it—and your face framed in the bonnet."

She could feel Mrs. Smith-Crompton's body quivering in fear. Yet she herself was no longer afraid of this spy, this Yankee monster, despite the great pistol that weighed in his hand.

"This is not your first season, I believe, Lady Diana?" he resumed.

"No, sir, my third."

"And you are but just engaged?"

"Two months ago."

"I should have married you at once, out of hand," he murmured regretfully. "I fear the British are somewhat slow. Still, perhaps the bride was reluctant."

There was a pause. She could not answer that. He was impudent—but he was keen. She had shown little concern over her fiancé's fate that night, and he knew it.

"Do you leave town soon, sir?" she asked politely.

A deep chuckle came from behind the dark cloak. "Too soon, my lady, I regret to say. I must return home. Would that you might go with me."

She bit her lips against saying that she would be traveling to America soon herself. How odd if they should meet in the new land. No, he was a spy, perhaps a member of some radical sect. An outlaw even!

"Have you been here long, sir?"

A slight hesitation. "Long enough, my lady. I long for home again, delightful though London shows itself to be. It has been most amusing—the theaters, the politics, I know not which is the better show!"

She could not keep back a little chuckle. Mrs. Smith-Crompton stiffened with horror. To banter with this—this outlaw, this spy! Diana must be mad!

"Indeed, sir. I trust you are aware that both my father and my fiancé are in politics?"

"Then how amusing a life you must lead, my lady!"

She shook with mirth, though she tried to conceal it. She had the feeling he could see her face, even in the darkness of the coach.

"And you, sir—is spying a regular—occupation with you?" she asked, when she could control her voice. It was icily formal once again.

"Not my regular occupation, my lady. Not so lively, but amusing enough. And you, what do you do all the day and evening?"

She hesitated. "Oh, I ride in the park, when in London. At home, in the country, I ride a great deal. And read. And oversee my father's house, and his entertainment."

"You would make a formidable hostess, I am sure. You entertain widely?"

"Constantly when in London. There are dinner parties in the evenings, cards in the afternoon. Your—sisters would perhaps enjoy them. And your wife."

"I have no wife, my lady, none to weep for me should I be caught. Should you weep for me?" he added softly, with a mocking inflection.

"You should weep for yourself, and reform your ways, sir," she said tartly.

He laughed. "There, I have met her but an hour, and she seeks to reform me. I have made a conquest, may I hope?" he said, in the mincing way of the London fops.

Even Mrs. Smith-Crompton gave a nervous little laugh.

"You do yourself too much honor, sir," said Diana sternly, but she found herself amazingly lighthearted at the knowledge that he was not married.

She was startled when the coach drew up suddenly. She peered out, to find herself at her own home. The footman came at once to draw down the steps and assist her out.

The pistol shone again in the light of the footman's torch. "I will keep the carriage, my lady, for a time." His voice was touched with hardness again.

Mrs. Smith-Crompton crawled out of the coach, shivering, and stood gazing anxiously toward them. Diana hissed, "You will harm Justin at your peril, sir! He has been with me for years! Take the carriage, as you will, but let him remain!"

"Softly, softly," he said, and helped her out. On the cobblestones, he gazed down at her. "You need not fear for him. He shall be home again in one hour, I promise you, safe and unharmed."

"If he is not—" she began.

He laughed softly, then raised her gloved hand and pressed a kiss to her fingers. "You need have no fear, I told you. He shall come home again. Drive on, Justin!" And boldly he jumped back into the carriage.

Justin stared down at his mistress, his plump face worried in the torchlight. Then he picked up the reins, and jogged the horses onward. The last she saw of the stranger was a hand waving from the window.

Diana turned on the footman, who stood with his mouth agape, and on her chaperone. "We shall go inside. And you will say nothing of this, nothing!" she told them fiercely.

The footman lighted them inside, and Diana hurried into a small drawing room where she flung off her cloak and went to the fire to warm herself. Looking up suddenly, she saw her face in the mirror, and stared.

Gone was the pale, languid face of an hour ago. Her eyes were brilliantly blue, as though a fire had been lit in them. Her face was flushed, her mouth scarlet without the aid of paint. She pressed her hands to her face, and it burned her fingers. She felt—alive, thrilled, as though compelled into some strange world she had not known existed.

Mrs. Smith-Crompton whispered, "Oh, dear, whatever shall we do? What will Lord Hubert say?"

Diana turned about slowly, striving for composure. "We will wait to see when Justin returns," she said. "Do retire, ma'am, I know you are weary."

The lady sat down in a chair with determination. Her face was lined with worry. "I will wait up with you, my lady."

"Very well." Diana slowly paced back and forth, watching the clock. The footman waited in the hallway. Once she went to the door, and he sprang to alertness. "My father has not yet returned?"

"No, my lady."

"Very well." She returned to her pacing. She sat down, but was too restless, too vibrant with new thoughts, to be still and calm. She paced again, watching the hands of the great golden clock move with painful slowness. One half hour, another fifteen minutes. Then the hour struck, two o'clock. It was exactly an hour since they had returned.

She was conscious of a deep disappointment. She had somehow trusted the word of that American, spy though he was. She should have known better.

It was then that the sound of a carriage came to her, the clop-clop of the weary horses' hooves. She sprang to the window and drew back the heavy silken draperies. She saw the footman hurry out with his torch, saw Justin get down. Another groom came to take the horses.

"He has returned!"

"Oh, thank God, thank God," breathed Mrs. Smith-Crompton.

Diana sped to the door to welcome Justin. She led the coachman into the small drawing room and firmly closed the door behind her before turning to question him.

"He let you go, as he said?"

"Oh, yes, mum, he be a true gentleman, he be." He gave her a little worried look. "Give me a gold coin, too, he did. Maybe I shouldn't ha' taken it?"

"No, no, keep it. Where did you leave him?" she asked eagerly.

He turned a dull red, and shuffled his great boots in embarrassment. "Oh, my lady, he made me swear I would not say," he said simply.

Diana stared at him. The stranger had such charm, he had even brought Justin under his spell. "No matter," she said briskly. "Justin, you and the footman must say nothing of this. Nothing! My reputation is at stake," she added impressively.

He promised earnestly that they would do nothing to injure her ladyship's reputation.

"And Father would be furious. When he comes home, say only that I have retired. Will you do as I ask?" She smiled at the footman, who eagerly assured her he would do whatever she said. "And do not gossip among yourselves about this. No word must leave this house. Please!"

When Lady Diana said "please," and added a bright smile, the servants did as she wished. With relief she went up to her bedroom. Her maid had instructions never to wait up for her past midnight, and the girl must be fast asleep. The fewer who knew of this, the better.

Diana lay down, weary, yet unable to sleep. Her mind went around and around. The charm of the man, the gay insolence of him! The kiss on her mouth. . . . She wondered at him. Were all spies so gay, so casual? Yet the pistol had lain ready at hand, the dagger up his sleeve.

She wondered about the papers stolen from the home of Prince Alexei. How damaging would they be, in American hands? But she soon forgot that, for thinking of the brazen, charming, daring American spy.

She had never met anyone like him. It was not that he was conventionally handsome; his bold face was too arrogant, his nose too long, his tan too deep a mahogany, he strode rather than walked. Yet he had grace—she had never danced with anyone who made her feel so light. He could have picked her up with one hand, she was convinced. When he had held his hand across her mouth, the other arm a band about her, she had felt as helpless as a babe.

She turned over restlessly in the bed, hearing the clocks chime three, then four o'clock. Did he not have a wife, then, or was he merely a charming liar? He had spoken of his sisters with affection. Her own brother would never have bothered to learn details of current fashions, only to relate them for her benefit. What kind of brother was he? Kind? Thoughtful? How many sisters did he have? Where did he live? What was his occupation, if he was not always a spy?

That deep tan of his must mean that he lived outdoors a great deal. She remembered then the feel of his cheek against hers, its hard warmth briefly scratching her tender cheek. She pressed her hand to her mouth. How hard and sweet his mouth had been. What had he thought of her? Would he call her "Lady Iceberg" as others had? He had not seemed to be repelled by her coldness or anger. His deep chuckle had answered her most biting remarks. A man among men, she thought, tucking her hand under her cheek to woo sleep.

But sleep did not come. Where was he now? Where had Justin left the man? No more than half an hour's drive from here. Where had he gone?

"Oh, this is ridiculous!" she muttered impatiently, getting up to walk about her room until the cold drove her back to the warm nest of blankets. "I shall forget him at once! I shall never see him again. A charming rogue, that is all! He is off to America—"

But what if they should meet in America? She smiled at that, a little foolishly, a little wistfully. She would be with her fiancé, and Geoffrey would scarcely appreciate a meeting with the man who had bested him.

It was dawn before she fell into a heavy sleep marred with nightmares, in which she was running and running, with a dark shadow behind her.

Chapter 3

Diana struggled out of the depths of sleep to hear her maid murmuring, "My lady? My lady? Will you be waking up soon now, my lady?"

She raised her heavy eyelids to see her maid bending anxiously over her.

"Oh—Hester." She yawned and stretched widely. "Is it very late?"

"Yes, my lady, gone twelve, it is. And Lord Hubert asking will you be coming down to lunch."

The strong note of worry in the maid's voice made Diana blink and force herself to sit up. "What's amiss?"

"Oh, he would be having you come down, my lady. Sir Geoffrey came early, he did, and they been talking for two hours. He'll be for lunch, also, but no others."

Diana sat and rubbed her eyes. The events of the last evening came sharply back to mind. Geoffrey was here, and furious, no doubt. Well, he would not take out his temper on her.

"Will you be wearing something grand?" The maid had gone over to the extensive wardrobes that lined one side of the room. She opened a door and gently touched the satins, the silks.

"No, the white muslin, the new one with the frills about the hem," said Diana. Today she would be demure, wide-eyed, and silent, she decided shrewdly.

Within the hour, she dressed in the white muslin, her hair brushed carefully into little curls about her forehead, and long sausage curls about her throat. Satisfied, she left her bedroom and slipped down the stairs to the great hall. As she approached her father's study, she could hear her fiancé's voice raised in anger: "An American spy— dammit all! It's a scandal!" Lord Hubert was attempting to soothe him.

Diana tapped lightly at the opened door. "May I interrupt your serious conversation?" she asked, and smiled brightly at them as she entered. "My apology for sleeping so late, Father!" She went over to brush her hand lightly on his sleeve. She rarely kissed him; he did not care for shows of affection.

Sir Geoffrey was flushed and red-rimmed of eye, as though he had slept little. He rose at her entrance, to bow deeply. "My apology for being forced to desert you last night, Diana," he said brusquely. "Events bore on me."

She thought of him in his lacy undergarments, and repressed a giggle. "Not at all, sir. We made our way home with our faithful coachman to watch over us. I trust all is well today?" she asked innocently.

He glared suspiciously at her wide blue eyes. She must take care, she thought. If he was not deceived by her explanation of her part in last night's events, he would question her as grimly as he would a remiss employee. But if she expressed too much concern for him, he might take it for a flirtatious advance on her part.

"What do you know of this matter of the spy, Diana?" asked her father, a worried frown between his graying eyebrows. "I hear you danced with the damned fellow!"

"He had on Geoffrey's jacket, Father, and I had no chance to see his face. I was completely fooled—until we parted at the door," she said demurely.

"Did you have a good look at his face then?" shot out Sir Geoffrey.

"I'm afraid not. It was dim there at the door."

"But you knew it was not I by that time?" he growled.

"Oh, yes, for his voice was not yours, when he finally spoke," she said hesitantly, raising a finger to her lips as if searching her memory. "Who was he? A spy, you said?"

"Damned American spy named Jeremy McCullough. Some sailor chap, brazen as all them are," said her father furiously. "Came right into London, wandered about free as you please. Well, we'll catch him today, that's certain. Geoffrey has seen his face, and we'll know him, right enough!"

Jeremy McCullough, she thought. Now she knew the name of the bold Yankee.

"What did he do last night? What was his purpose?" she inquired.

"Stole some papers from the Russians," said her

father briefly. "Now, you'll know no more about it, Diana! Such matters are not for females."

"Of course not, Papa," she said. Not for females indeed! she thought rebelliously. Females must provide entertainment, must choose the men's food and wines, must always be pretty. But she must not use her mind, must not question their decisions concerning her. Even her engagement to Geoffrey had taken place without the merest question concerning her own wishes.

Oh, what was the matter with her! Life was like this for females, at least in England. She knew that well enough. At least she had some education, for her governess had taught her well in languages, mathematics, literature, music. And the world envied her the fiancé her father had chosen.

A footman came in to announce luncheon, and she went in on her father's arm, to sit silent at the foot of the table, keeping alert for any tidbits of information.

The conversation finally turned from the spy to their proposed trip to America. The trade mission was discussed earnestly. The Americans must be made to see the advantage of exporting more raw materials—hemp, cotton, wool—to England, to be traded for finished goods. Their ideas of building mills of their own, the better to process their own materials, must be discouraged. They had not the skills of mother England. Tobacco was a valuable product also, and the Americans would be wooed with higher prices for the good crops of their southern fields.

Sir Geoffrey was evidently calmer by the time he had consumed half a dozen courses of soup, fish, beef, pudding, cheese, pastry. In a more mellow mood, he turned to his fiancée, and patted her hand.

"And now, my dear, have you nearly completed your wardrobe for the journey? You have no doubt recalled that you will need warm cloaks, yet very smart? And bonnets in the latest fashion. We count on you to overwhelm both the ladies and the gentlemen in the colonies, and I have every confidence in your ability to do so."

"I will be going to my dressmaker this afternoon, sir, for some final fittings. I trust you will not be disappointed in my taste."

Her father frowned. The mention of dressmakers made him unhappy, for they presented such huge bills. However, within six months his daughter would be married, and her bills would be paid by her husband. That was a happy thought. Then he could concentrate on the matter of a proper marriage of his only son. He had been seriously considering several fine females, with titles and with fortunes—a happy task. His son was intelligent, handsome, considered a fine hand with horses. What more could a female wish? What more could her father wish, which was more to the point. Yes, as soon as they returned from America and got Diana married off, he could put his best efforts to securing a good match for Thomas. The lad did not wish marriage—he was having too good a time—but good times need not end. Naturally the boy would take a mistress, after he had done his family duties, of course.

After luncheon, Sir Geoffrey escorted Diana and her maid to the dressmaker's. Mrs. Smith-Crompton had a vile headache, and Diana had persuaded her to remain in bed. She thought secretly that the woman had had a bad fright, and that the longer she remained away from the rest of the household, the less possibility there was of the good woman's blurting out what had happened.

The dressmaker was in high good humor. Some new materials had been smuggled in from France, and she showed them to Diana eagerly.

"You will appreciate the beauty of this silver and blue fabric, the finest silk, my lady! I long to turn it into a ballgown for you. And here is some taffeta—" She spread out the fabric with loving hands, and the shimmering pink and gray stripes flowed over her arm.

"Ahhh—it is beautiful." An imp of mischief overcame Diana. She ordered the new fabrics lavishly. Her father would sell her, would he? Well then, he would pay handsomely for his pains.

A twinge of unhappiness lurked beneath that mischief. She did not want to marry. Being under a father's thumb was bad enough. To exist under Geoffrey's cold rule would be infinitely worse, for there would be no escaping that.

She returned home with a carriage full of new garments, including three new bonnets, and had left behind her enough orders to keep the dressmaker busy until Diana's departure for America.

Before going down to tea, she stole softly to her companion's rooms. They were in dimness, and Mrs. Smith-Crompton lay in her bed, weeping softly into a pillow. She tried to hide her tears when Diana entered, but Diana's heart was touched at once.

"My dear," she said affectionately, anxiously drawing up a chair beside the bed. "What is it? Is your head much worse? Shall I send for a physician? Tell me!"

"No, no, it is not that. Forgive me, please, my lady."

"But you are not treating me as a friend and relative," Diana coaxed. "What is it? Your fright last night?" she added softly.

Mrs. Smith-Crompton dabbed a handkerchief over her face. She sniffed. Her graying hair was spread out over the pillow, the mobcap having come awry.

"Oh, my lady, you will think me so ungrateful. It was a shock to me, and I fear it has unhinged me. But I was thinking about my own—future, my lady. When you are married, you see."

"Yes—of course," said Diana, mentally berating herself. She had cringed so fiercely from the thought of her own future that she had not thought of the future of her relative either.

"You will not—need me after your marriage. I was wondering— Oh, dear, whatever will become of me!" Weak sobs shook her frame. She was a nervous, timid woman at the best of times. The thought of going out into the world again, penniless and alone, shook her badly.

Diana was thinking rapidly. She asked, "What would you do if you could do anything you pleased?" She had sometimes asked herself that very question, in bitter, futile moments.

"Oh, I would ask nothing more than to have a position with a lady such as yourself," said Mrs. Smith-Crompton, nervously dabbing at her eyes.

"No, no, I mean if you could do anything at all. Have a house of your own—live where you please—"

A gleam came into the gentle eyes. "Oh, a cottage by the sea, a dear little cottage all my own, and the sound of the sea in my ears," she said dreamily. "And roses growing by the walk, and my own little chickens—" She paused abruptly, flushing. "Dear me, what must you think of me!"

Diana patted her hand, much relieved. She did not see why Mrs. Smith-Crompton should not have her dream—such an easy dream to fulfill. "I'll see what I can do," she said decisively. "I'll speak to Papa, for after all, I shall not need a chaperone after I marry, shall I? And I shall be away six months—"

In a new and strange land, where anything could happen, where bold, tanned seamen turned into spies and laughingly stole kisses.

"Oh, I should not have said anything," began the woman, brightening up amazingly. "But I have so worried about the future—"

Diana patted her hand reassuringly, then went down to tea. She served charmingly, smiled at her guests, made the proper quips and responses, and was vastly relieved when they all departed. Her father stretched out before the fire, quite satisfied.

"Papa, I shall not need a companion when I marry, shall I?" she asked.

"Hm? Oh, no, no, of course not. Your husband by your side, and so on," muttered Lord Hubert, already thinking about how to win a conservative lord over to his side of an important issue. The man was fond of hunting. He would offer him his shooting box for the autumn—wouldn't be here to use it anyway.

"So Mrs. Smith-Crompton should be provided for," said Diana softly. "I thought a little cottage by the sea might be nice."

"Um, yes, yes, of course. Settle it with Perkins," he said. "Have to see to some matters, my dear, if you'll excuse me. You'll be dining at home this evening?"

"Yes, Geoffrey is bringing several guests. At about seven, Papa," she reminded him, then went to his study, where she found Perkins, his loyal solicitor. She explained Mrs. Smith-Crompton's needs: a cottage by the sea and a generous pension of about three hundred pounds a year.

"Are you sure your father is agreeable?" asked the man, amazed.

"Oh, yes, we have just discussed it," said Diana sunnily.

And so it was settled. Lord Hubert fumed a little when he heard the full terms, but Diana as-

sured him earnestly that he had agreed to it. And
plans were proceeding so rapidly for the journey
to America, he had plenty to think about besides
his daughter's companion. Diana had counted on
that.

Sir Geoffrey came often to the Somerville town
house as the time approached for them to depart.
He found no fault with his fiancée, who was a
beautiful hostess, gay and gracious to his guests,
but very proper in her manners. All envied him,
and his chest swelled with pride in her. At the
same time, he could not help but worry at her
continuing coldness to his advances.

"Shy," said Lord Hubert. "Her mother was like
that at first. You'll find she'll warm up when you
marry her."

Sir Geoffrey took heart and made bold one evening to put his arm about Diana's waist as they
were momentarily alone in the drawing room. "Do
you realize, my sweet, we shall be married in six
months?"

He felt her give a distinct shudder, and she re-
treated from him warily. "But we are not married
yet, sir. Pray, do not!" She backed away again as
he came forward.

"Oh, nonsense, girl, you are cold as an icicle!
Time to warm you up?" He laughed uneasily. He
was becoming impatient with her. Why, he was
leaving behind a charming little ballerina to accompany Diana and Lord Hubert to America. She
ought to appreciate his sacrifice . . . though of
course she must never learn of it.

He caught her to himself and attempted to kiss her. She turned her head, presenting only her cheek to him. He touched it with his lips.

She restrained another shudder. He had been drinking, and the smell of brandy was heavy on his breath. And she abhorred the wet touch of his mouth on her face. She moved away as soon as he lifted his head.

"Wait till we are married," he said significantly, as she drew away from him. "You'll sing a different tune then."

"I am not accustomed to embraces," she said lightly. "You would not have me a loose woman, I think?"

"Don't be nonsensical! I know you are not; you are always the perfect lady," he said. "However, you should show more warmth to me. Or are you cold all the way through?" And his gaze went down over her creamy-white silk dress, over the low-cut bosom and the slim waist, the soft folds of the dress over her hips, to her slim feet in white slippers. "Cold as snow, you look," he said, a little angrily. "Why don't you wear something brighter?"

"These clothes please me. After—after we are married, you may choose my clothing, I suppose, sir," she said, and felt a distinct chill travel down her spine.

"And pay your bills, too, I expect. Though your father has promised you a good dowry," he added idly. Presently he took his leave, with relief on his part as well as hers, she thought.

She lay awake again that night. She wondered

sometimes what had happened to the Yankee spy, Jeremy McCullough. He seemed scarcely more real than a figure in a dream, or in a drama which had never happened. Yet when she closed her eyes, she could feel the warmth of his mouth against hers, the hardness of his body against her soft one. And she had not felt disgusted.

May drew to a close. Huge trunks stood in her drawing room, filled to bursting with gowns, cloaks, parasols, gloves, stoles, spencers, slippers. Huge hatboxes were filled with bonnets of the latest mode, huge-brimmed, with long ribbons, in all her favorite shades of blue, pink, and silver. Hester worked eagerly to have everything ready for her mistress, but confessed to a growing apprehension over the sea voyage. Though proud that she had been chosen to accompany Lady Diana, she worried constantly about being seasick, or falling overboard, or being shot at by Indians.

June came, and great carriages arrived to be loaded with trunks and cases, valises and hatboxes, crates of blankets and sheets and pillows, all the household items they would need for the voyage and the months in America. It was finally time to depart.

Mrs. Smith-Crompton thanked Diana again and again for the little cottage by the sea, and departed thankfully for it. She would sit out her days on her own porch, tending her roses, with a comfortable pension paid to her monthly, and no worries ever again, she said. Diana hoped that life would indeed be so kind to the good woman.

Diana departed from London on a chilly, raw June day, with the rain beating down steadily from an overcast sky. The day was no gloomier than her mood, however, as she thought of six months in close company with her fiancé.

It was a long drive down to the port, and dusk had long since fallen by the time the carriages began to pull up beside the smart frigate, the *Ulysses,* which was to carry them. Diana descended from the carriage and stared up at the ship's black-painted sides with a cold feeling in her heart.

It was so huge, its tall masts reaching up to the sky, and the curious seamen staring down at her. She heard her father talking briskly to a smartly uniformed man. Guessing him to be the captain, she drew near to be introduced.

She smiled at Captain Sir Arnold Talbot, and he bent over her hand. The red-faced man beamed at her. "Glad to have you aboard, my lady. I hope we have a smooth sailing for you!"

"What's this about men jumping ship?" Sir Geoffrey asked irritably. After the tiresome journey he was dusting off his jacket fastidiously, and had scarcely paused to shake hands with the captain. "How dare they? Have you obtained more men?"

"No, sir, sorry, sir. A Navy ship came in before us and they seem to have found every able-bodied man in the city," replied the captain apologetically. They were still discussing the shortage of seamen as he escorted them aboard and to their cabins.

Diana stood in the midst of her tiny cabin, with another small cabin next door for her maid, and wished she could weep. Her throat felt thick with unshed tears. She was leaving her homeland for the open sea and an unknown country. And she was afraid.

But even more terrifying than the unknown was the prospect of being in such close quarters with a man she knew only too well. She wished she could also jump ship—but they would only find her again. There was no escape.

Chapter 4

Hester unpacked enough clothing for the voyage, and Diana paced the deck in a smart blue serge gown with a cloak of blue velvet, and a bonnet tied securely over her curls. She took amazingly to the sea, and found the crisp wind welcome to her face, the informal life aboard ship even more welcome.

Sir Geoffrey took bravely to it as well, and paced the deck with her every morning and evening. She could almost like him aboard the *Ulysses*, she thought, for he relaxed somewhat from his anxious role of diplomat. He told stories of his early days with the Navy, and of some piratical adventures in the West Indies. Perhaps marriage could be tolerable after all, thought Diana—except when he attempted to kiss her in some dark corner of the ship. She always managed to break away after a brief kiss on her cheek. He did not press her further—perhaps on her father's advice, she thought.

Lord Hubert remained in his cabin much of the time, going over papers. Captain Talbot occupied himself with the ship, no easy task with the shortage of seamen. It seemed that some impressed men from American ships had mysteriously disappeared while they were in harbor. One night they had been safely aboard, the next morning they were gone, and no one knew where.

One morning, about five days out to sea, the lookout sighted a ship in the distance. Diana was walking with Sir Geoffrey, and they paused to stare at the western horizon.

"Sail ahoy!" called the seaman perched high in the rigging. "West by southwest!"

Sir Geoffrey came alert. "I wonder if it might be one of those damned Yankee ships," he muttered. He excused himself hastily to Diana, and left her standing at the railing, leaning forward eagerly to watch as they closed the gap between the *Ulysses* and the other ship.

Suddenly crewmen were dashing all over the deck. One seaman muttered to another, "Might be that Yankee brig we sighted afore we left the harbor. Wonder if he dared hang about!"

"Slower ship, we mighta caught up with 'im," murmured his friend. They both stared with keen eyes into the distance.

Diana saw Captain Talbot appear and raise a spyglass to his eye. He stared, muttering to himself. Behind him, Geoffrey urged, "Is it an American ship, sir? Is it?"

"Cannot tell yet, sir. Would you have a look?" And he handed over the spyglass. Geoffrey raised it to his eye, then finally lowered it with a sigh.

"I can't tell either. We shall have to get closer. If it is a Yankee ship, we must attack. We could certainly use their crew aboard the *Ulysses!*"

Talbot gave Diana a worried look. "But, sir,

with the ladies aboard—it would be different if her ladyship was not with us. We cannot take the risk—"

"Nonsense. Diana can go below. You surely cannot expect a pack of Yankees to give our men much of a fight?" Sir Geoffrey said scornfully.

Lord Hubert came up from his cabin and looked out to sea with interest. "A Yankee, eh? Well, this should be interesting. I wonder what she carries. Stolen goods, no doubt."

Diana was biting her lip, wondering if she dared interfere. Geoffrey was urging Captain Talbot to attack. Her father seemed indifferent, but the captain was definitely worried.

Finally Diana said cautiously, "But would you attack the ship merely to acquire more men? To impress them? I thought that was the weight of the argument in the colonies—I mean, the former colonies? That they are angry at the impressment of their citizens?"

All three men looked at her with the patient, rather glazed expression she had often noticed when she attempted to enter their conversations.

"My dear Diana," said Sir Geoffrey, "do not trouble yourself over it. We are but recovering our own men, who desert at the least hint of work. It is a fact that most of the men we impress from their ships turn out to be English citizens, not Americans. Besides, are not the Americans really British?" He shrugged, and took up the spyglass again.

The ship came closer. They watched, taking

turns with the long spyglass, growing excited as the lookout called down that he thought it was indeed a Yankee brig. He called out the number of her guns: "Twenty-two, sir, I believe! and her sails limp. She may be injured!"

Sir Geoffrey grew more excited and hurried below, to return quickly in full uniform of scarlet and gold, his sword belted to his waist. Lord Hubert did likewise, and made a grand entrance, a pistol added to his uniform. Captain Talbot then called for the clearing of the decks.

The men began to run about in what looked to Diana like mysteriously well-ordered frenzy. Huge guns were wheeled out, and the crew had armed themselves with knives and pistols. The marines came up on the double, smartly clad in scarlet, their hats cocked, their faces red with excitement.

Diana was escorted below to her cabin by Sir Geoffrey, who seemed in a hurry to be rid of her. She tried one more protest.

"I do not believe you should attack the ship, Geoffrey, for such a reason," she said earnestly. "It will but give them one more excuse to be angry with England. Is our mission not sufficiently important to pacify them? We do not want to rouse still more anger, by impressing more of their seamen."

"You do not comprehend political matters, Diana," he said curtly. "I have already explained to you that the men aboard are probably our own men. We shall return them eventually to England, after some sea duty has cleared their heads."

And he was gone, leaving her to the charge of her wide-eyed maid. Hester was trembling with fear. "Oh, my lady, whatever are they about?" she breathed.

"Going to attack," said Diana with a deep sigh. "Oh, men! Forever at war! When will they learn it is sheer foolishness? We go on a peaceful mission to the colonies, but all will be lost when we attack one of their ships. If only—" She stopped and bit her lip at the amazed stare of her maid. She went to the small porthole to gaze out.

The Yankee brig was closer, much closer. And all her sails hung limp as the swift British frigate drew up to her. Diana shook her head. The poor Americans—injured already, probably from another battle.

Lord Hubert popped in the door, his face crimson with excitement. "She *is* Yankee," he said importantly. "And injured at that. Shouldn't last long, Diana. Keep your head covered, and don't come up on any account! We'll have them licked in a trice!"

And he was gone again, pounding up the stairs like a man half his age.

"Oh, my lady!" cried Hester, "we'd best hide under the beds!" Frantically she flung herself to the floor and crawled under the small bed, her long legs sticking out ridiculously. Her weeping was punctuated by anguished moans.

Diana stayed at the porthole, her hands clasped tightly. She heard the crisp shouted orders, heard the pounding of feet on the deck, then the rattle as the guns were rolled out. The whole ship shook as the first round was fired.

She heard Captain Talbot's voice boom out across the waves: "Do you yield? Strike your colors!"

From her angle, Diana could see the strange ship clearly. She was smaller than their frigate, her sails still limp. But even as she watched and listened for a call from across the waters, she stiffened. For the sails of the Yankee brig suddenly sprang full! They billowed into the wind, and she came swiftly forward. Her colors showed boldly now—the colors of the Americans, red, white, and blue. How ironic, Diana thought, that they still shared England's colors. Her name showed clearly as the brig came aside—*Eagle*—and her port, *Boston*. Diana clenched her hands with excitement.

Then she cringed, and the full force of a blast knocked her off her feet. She found herself sitting on the floor of the cabin, rubbing her head. The *Eagle* had opened up the frigate *Ulysses* with a full cannonade across her, raking her as she passed!

Shouts, screams of encouragement, then of agony as some were injured. Diana forced herself up again, to find from the porthole that the *Eagle* had sailed past, so close she could make out the faces of the seamen on the other brig. They bent to their heavy guns, and another load was poured into the cannons' great black maws.

On board, she could see the figures of some men firing steadily into the deck of the *Ulysses*.

One man stood out, clad in a blue coat with buff lapels, white knee breeches, and stock. She saw the gleam of gold on his shoulders. Now he was taking off his cocked black hat and waving it imperiously.

Odd—she thought he looked like that Yankee spy. That Jeremy McCullough. Did all Yankees look like that, with bronze hair, a tall, sturdy frame, a tan from the wind and the sun?

Then the *Eagle* was past them, and turning about in the wind. More shots were fired, and the *Ulysses* shuddered under her feet. The guns below her were firing in a steady round, from front to back of the ship, one after another. She clung to the bedpost, and gazed wide-eyed as the *Eagle* came about and swept down the entire length of the British ship.

There was a great rending tear as the mast tore through the rigging of the *Ulysses*, and crashed to the deck. On deck, Geoffrey was waving his sword. His pistol, now emptied, was flung aside. "Fight on, boys," he yelled hoarsely. "Fight on, we'll have them! Fight on! Give them another volley!"

The crackle of musketry sounded again, and Diana clapped her hands over her ears as the *Eagle* answered with more muskets. The shots were deafening her. What must it be like on deck? she wondered in horror.

Another great cry came up. She uncovered her ears to listen.

"They are boarding us! They are boarding—

More men on deck! More men on deck—load your rifles— More grape in the guns—"

The orders became confused, nearly drowned out by the screaming and the pounding of feet. Diana grew cold with apprehension. Hester still wept under the bed.

"Come out, Hester," said Diana, firmly. "I think—I think the battle is not going our way!"

"My God, we will all be murdered in our beds," moaned Hester. Diana bent down to reassure her.

"Come out, Hester, we won't be murdered in our beds if we are not in them. Come out; where is your pistol?"

"I don't know, my lady—I don't know—"

Well, it would not do much good anyway. Diana found her little dagger, strapped it to her wrist, tested the ease with which she could pull it from the left arm. Then she returned to the window.

She could see nothing now. The British frigate was turning about, trying to take advantage of the wind in her favor. But sails were strewn about the deck—Diana could see them hanging down over the sides of the ship.

"Strike your colors to us!" called a clear, strong voice.

"Be damned to you!" Geoffrey shouted in reply. Confusion followed as Captain Talbot barked out that he was in command of this vessel.

Another volley of heavy guns answered their arguing. When it ended, Diana felt the strong frigate *Ulysses* shuddering to a halt. And another call chilled her blood.

"Hit below the waterline!" someone yelled. "We're taking on water fast!"

"Strike your colors!" came the clear yell once more. "You're flooding! Strike! We must take you aboard!"

Captain Talbot yelled in reply, "We strike! For God's sake, help us! We're going down already!"

Heavy thumping steps, a clatter, a rush of confused sound, and then stamping boots were heard outside Diana's door. It was pushed open, and Lord Hubert stood there, his sword hanging from his hand, his heavy face pale.

"Come, Diana, we must go up," he said quietly. "We are taken, and the ship is going down."

"Yes, Father." She hauled up her maid by one arm, grabbed up her jewel box, and forced her maid to accept a valise. She stuffed in a few clothes and pushed Hester ahead of her. Her father waited impatiently, glancing back over his shoulder.

He urged the two ladies up on deck, ahead of him. His valet stood there, holding Lord Hubert's own jewel box; his long, mournful face was full of shock. Diana glanced about, and thought she would faint at the gruesome scene before her.

Men lay on the deck, covered with their own crimson blood. One man clutched at the stump of his bloodied arm, his head lolling in unconsciousness. Blood covered the deck, and grapeshot, and other spent ammunition from the American ship. She could scarcely find a place to set her feet.

Wide-eyed, she stared at the myriad of ropes and fragile planks connecting the two ships. Across the planks ran fleet-footed American sailors, some barefoot. And on the other side, directing them all, a tall, bronze-haired man.

Sir Geoffrey stood sullenly, his sword pointed to the ground. A sailor came up to him jauntily, and took the sword from him. Lightly, the American captain ran across the planks and jumped down to survey the scene. Sir Arnold came up to him, squared his shoulders, and handed his sword to the man.

"I am Captain Sir Arnold Talbot. May I compliment you, sir, on a magnificent fight?" His face was pale but for a streak of blood from a wound across the cheek.

The other captain bowed briefly. "There is no time for conversation, sir. Get your men over to my ship at once. Yours is going down speedily. We can take on all your men, I think. Get what food stores you can, though. Ours are not enough for the lot we'll be carrying."

He turned his head, and Diana saw his face clearly. It was the Yankee spy, serious now, not jaunty or amused. His green eyes blazed at her; he did not seem to know her.

But Sir Geoffrey came up to him at once. "Why, it's that damned Yankee spy I caught in Prince Alexei's house, stealing papers!" he cried, outraged. "Are you a pirate, then?"

"No, sir, a privateer only," said the man, mockingly. "I have no time for you now. If you will but get aboard the *Eagle*—"

"He is a damned pirate!" repeated Sir Geoffrey. "He is no honest ship's captain!"

"I am captain of the *Eagle* and you are my prisoners," said the man flatly. "If you dispute this, we shall consider the matter later! For now, your ship is sinking. If you wish to live, get aboard mine!"

Sir Geoffrey glared at him, then backed away sullenly. Forgetting all else, he scrambled up onto the rail, walked across the planks separating the two ships, and disappeared over the side, where a man in a red headscarf greeted him. Diana lost sight of him, standing silent with her jewel box and her trembling maid.

Captain McCullough was giving crisp orders. Seamen ran this way and that. Food stores were carried over the planks and dumped down on the deck of the *Eagle*. The two captains conferred gravely, and gave swift orders, so that as much gear as possible might be transferred.

Several seamen were ordered by Captain McCullough to attend to the wounded who lay half-conscious on the deck. Each huge sailor gathered up one of the men, and carried him deftly across the planks, somehow balancing their considerable weight on the thin passageway between the two ships. More bloodied men were carried up from below, where they had been injured as they tended the great guns.

Diana felt forgotten, standing there with her maid in the shadows of the broken spars and masts. She saw her father come up with more of his own gear, his valet helping carry the trunks and valises. He piled them on the deck and went below again for more. Captain McCullough glanced at Diana, waiting so gravely, and gave a crisp order to two seamen. They ran below and began returning with some of her trunks and boxes.

She felt dazed. The crack of the guns still echoed in her head. She reeled from the horrid sights of the injured ship—the bloody men, one man with his eye gone, one with his arm blown from his body. Had it been worth it, to fight like that? And for whom?

The deck of the ship gave a lurch, and the *Ulysses* sank lower in the water.

The deck was swarming now with American seamen trying to speed the movement of people and gear toward the *Eagle*. The captain of the *Ulysses* waited at the side, his face tortured as he watched his ship going down, his feet braced to take the lurching of the frigate.

It was all a frightful nightmare. Diana thought of her father's confidence, of Sir Geoffrey urging on the attack. It would all be over quickly, they had said. Yes, it had been over quickly, but the Yankee had won. The Yankee who now stood aboard the crippled *Ulysses*, swiftly and boldly in command.

Chapter 5

A man called across the narrow stretch of waters that separated the two ships. "The hull be full, Cap'n! Best come aboard! She be sinking fast; the water is rushing in!"

"Right!" called Captain McCullough. He motioned to Diana and her maid. "Come aboard, ladies. Welcome to the *Eagle!*"

Both women stared frozenly at the thin planks. The captain grinned, then motioned to two sturdy seamen about to cross over. "Take the maid with you, men. Close your eyes," he said encouragingly to the pallid Hester, who was clutching the valise to her body. "They'll guide you across." He gave her a push. When she stumbled, he lifted her bodily to the plank, and gave her into the care of the first burly seaman. "Shut your eyes!" he ordered, and Hester did so. She was steered across the narrow planks, and let down the other side.

Diana swallowed and went up to the railing. She must go also, but how—how—Behind her the captain came up. He stood behind her. "Come along, my lady. No hesitation now," he said brusquely.

She nodded. She felt sick with fear, but she must not show it. So many were watching her.

Then the captain swept her up into his arms, as

though she weighed no more than a feather. He leaped up onto the planks, which swayed dangerously, fearsomely, beneath his feet.

"Shut your eyes," he said bluntly. But she could not; she stared up at his lean, tanned face, and in a trice she was across the planks. For a moment he gazed down at her, his face grave. Then he dumped her down onto the deck of the *Eagle*, and was up on the planks again, and back to the other ship.

"This way, my lady," said a seaman, respectfully tugging his forelock. "I'll show you to the captain's quarters."

"The captain's quarters!" she gasped, outraged. Did he think she would share his quarters with him? She looked about wildly for her father, for Geoffrey. They were not in sight.

She stood there, stubbornly refusing to move. Hester was nearby, quivering with fright. Then the captain came back, urging Captain Talbot with him.

"We must away," he was saying. "The wash of the ship may cause us to lurch and take water. Come along, sir; no more can be done."

"Yes, yes, you are right. But, my God, to lose my ship—" There was agony in the British captain's voice.

"Fortunes of war!" said McCullough, with cheerful callousness. "You would attack me, sir!"

"Yes, yes—" muttered Captain Talbot. They climbed down, the last to leave the *Ulysses*. Diana shrank back into the shadow of a torn sail, with Hester at her side.

"Cut her loose!" called Captain McCullough. Seamen ran to lift down the planks and unfasten the ropes that tied the *Eagle* to the sinking vessel. The Yankee captain watched alertly, hands on his lean hips. He sprang up to the quarterdeck and gave crisp orders to his men.

The ship moved away slowly, another sail was hoisted, and they drew clear of the *Ulysses*. Captain Talbot stood at the railing, and as they drew away he raised his hand in a long salute to his wretched vessel.

Diana watched also, fascinated. The ship was like a crippled sea animal, groaning in its pain. She turned sideways in the waters, and the wind moaned through the rags of her rigging. They drew away more swiftly. From across the widening gap of waters, she saw the British vessel turn in the waters, and with incredible swiftness she sank, the sea gurgling about her black hull, the tall masts disappearing from sight until all that was left was the top of one mast. Then that also was gone, and the waters closed over her.

Captain Talbot finally turned away, his face grim. Diana saw the look, as that of a man watching a beloved wife buried. His shoulders were drooping, his head bent.

He held to the rail. Captain McCullough turned over the ship to another man, then leaped down again and went to Talbot.

"Come, sir, I'll show you to your quarters." He

turned about, and noticed Diana and Hester waiting. His mouth quirked. "What, watching the sinking? Have you seen nothing like it before, my lady?"

"I have never been at sea before, sir," she said faintly.

"Well, well, this has been an adventure for you," he said gravely, but that mocking twinkle was in his bold green eyes. "Now, I'll show you to my quarters—"

He touched her arm, to indicate the way. She shrank from him. She gave him a cold look. "I do not know, sir, what you intend. But I'll have none of your quarters! My father—"

He stared at her, then flung back his head and laughed aloud, a merry, ringing laugh. "Oh, come, my lady! I would not seduce a lady in the very presence of her father. Think better of me than that. I'll bunk with my lieutenant." And he gently pushed her toward the stairs.

A great wave of relief came over her. She felt a fool, but a happy one. She went silently where he indicated. He showed her and Hester into a neat small cabin with two bunks, and a desk fastened to the wall. She looked about curiously.

"My men have not had time to clear out my gear. Forgive us, my lady," he said, with mock gravity. "I'll send a man for it presently. Meanwhile, I must return to my duties." He gave her a formal bow.

She curtsied without thinking, and was glad when the door closed to shut out his gleaming eyes and amused mouth. Hester gave a great sigh. "I feared we would be murdered," she said. "He seems a gentleman, does he not, my lady?"

"He has the manners of one," said Lady Diana.

Soon a tapping at the door heralded the arrival of one of the seamen, who blushed as he apologized for his entrance, and began efficiently to gather up the captain's gear.

They were fine clothes, Diana observed—splendid blue uniforms and soft white shirts. And a strange golden object, which the seaman handled as reverently as a chalice, something to do with the sea, thought Diana. He packed it all up briskly, and left after clearing enough space for her maid to unpack a trunk and a valise for Diana, and some clothing for herself.

Lord Hubert tapped, and came in to glance about in some surprise and dissatisfaction. "Ah, you have the best cabin, I see," he murmured. "I have but a cubicle for myself and my valet, and Geoffrey the same."

"The captain was most kind," said Diana gravely, wondering if she should give up her cabin to her father.

"I'm down with the officers, wouldn't do for you at all," sighed Lord Hubert. "But I shall be most uncomfortable. I mean to request that he turn back and land us in England. We cannot proceed now, of course."

"You mean, since you have wrecked your mission, Papa?" asked Diana innocently. He gave her a scowl.

"Nonsense, nothing like that. He would not hold that against us. I talked to Captain Talbot. He stated firmly that several of the *Eagle's* seamen were on his ship originally. The Yankee has stolen them from us. So we were perfectly justified in attacking."

Men had strange ways of reasoning, thought Diana, but was too wise to say so.

Her father left her, to return to his "cubicle," and she discarded her velvet cloak and went up on deck. There she found the many wounded seamen still lying about, stretched out on rags made from useless sails. Two men were going about, tending to them. She approached the elder of the men.

"Sir, I have some knowledge of medicine. If I can be of some assistance—" She flinched from the sight of the wounds, but could not refrain from offering.

" 'Tis not work for you, my lady," said the man kindly, brushing back his hair with his arm. His hands were bloody.

"I would help, if I could," she insisted. She knelt on the other side of the man who lay limply between them, his eyes closed. "I could take care of this wound on his face, if you will but give me ointment and cloths."

The man gave her a keen look, noted her pale face and resolute chin. "Well, my lady, don't know what the captain would say—" He gave her a cheeky grin, and handed across some cloths and a pot of greasy-smelling ointment.

Gently she dabbed at the man's cheek. He

opened his eyes and stared at her. "Coo, an angel," he murmured, and shut his eyes wearily again.

The other man chuckled, binding up the arm. The man had lost his arm below the elbow. "Thought it would bring him out of it," he said. "Ain't seen a real lady for months, he ain't."

Then he was silent for a time, adjusting the bandages. When he and Diana were finished, he beckoned to a burly seaman, who picked up the man and carried him below.

"Will he be cared for down there?" asked Diana doubtfully, wiping her hands on a cloth.

"Oh, aye, my lady. The captain will see to it. Might I introduce meself, seeing we're working together? I am Eli Ulrich, first mate to the captain."

He had a kindly, ruddy face, and as he stood up she observed his long, lanky frame. Diana also rose and shook his hand smilingly. She liked the warm, friendly gleam in his eyes.

"Lady Diana Somerville, Mr. Ulrich."

"You'll please me if you call me Eli. They all does," he said. He turned to another man, waiting on the deck nearby. He knelt down beside him, and again Diana knelt on the other side. This man was more gravely wounded, gasping for breath, his hand pressed to his ribs.

Eli Ulrich unfastened the torn and ragged shirt. Gently he eased the cloth from the wound in the belly. His face turned grave. "A nasty one, miss; you'd best not look."

"If he can endure it, I can look upon it," she said bravely, though she felt sick at the sight. She handed fresh cloths to him, thanked a young seaman when he brought a bucket of fresh water. She helped wash and salve the wound, and fasten a thick cloth over it. The man groaned when he was lifted to be carried below, and his head fell back as the seaman carried him below.

They moved on to another man, a British seaman who watched with suspicion as the Yankee bent over him. He knew Lady Diana, however, and watched her worriedly as she helped examine the wound in his leg. "It be nasty, miss?" he inquired, in a thin, exhausted voice.

"It looks bad, but we shall do our best for you," she said steadily, and held his shoulders firmly with her young arms as Eli Ulrich had to wrench at the leg to straighten it. He gasped, and fell back unconscious.

"Broken clean through the skin," muttered Eli, shaking his head. "Splint it, we will."

"Are you a doctor, then—Eli?" she ventured, watching him work deftly.

"Ah, no, my lady. All of us has to know something of medicines on the ship. The captain, he be best at it."

He nodded toward the other side of the ship. Diana turned about from her crouch on the deck. To her surprise, she saw the Yankee captain bending over a British sailor, as he worked on a wound in the lower thigh. Diana watched as he probed gently, and the man cried out.

"Easy, man," Jeremy McCullough said calmly. " 'Twill take but an instant more. Easy, hold still—" He nodded to another seaman, who bent to hold the man down. A quick probe, and the man cried out again. But McCullough held up a fragment of shot triumphantly. Then he cleaned and swabbed the wound, and bandaged him. The British sailor was taken below.

"Will—they take care with him?" Diana asked in a low voice. "Just as they would for your own men?"

Eli gave her a penetrating look, and she was ashamed. "Of course, my lady," he said quietly. "The captain is a good man. None better. He don't take it out on fallen foe, he don't."

"Pardon me, I should not have asked," she said.

He gave her a smile of understanding. "There, now, miss, you can't know him. Me, I've sailed with Jeremy lad for nigh on ten years, since he first signed on as a young sprig. Learns his way, he does, then buys his own ship, and runs her like the Navy, he does."

"Oh—he is not in the American Navy, then?" she asked timidly. She hungered strangely to hear more of the bold Yankee. "He said something about a privateer. What is that?"

Eli sat back to study the next man's wound, a nasty one on his left leg. "Well, miss," he said absently, "we ain't got enough ships to do us in the Navy, not since President Jefferson, he said to cut back. But we got a fine merchant navy, we have. Mr. McCullough's father is a shipbuilder, and all the lads are in the ships, you see. We takes on cargo, and goes where she goes. Of late, it's all over the Atlantic. And with the British always trying to impress our seamen, we have to have the means to defend ourselves."

She flushed for shame, for she had just witnessed such an incident; Geoffrey had shown no reluctance about trying to impress American men. "I can understand that. But does your government approve of what you do?"

"Oh, miss, they would not last, but for us," he said, a gleam of pride in his eyes. "They gives us letters of marque, and we sail for the government, and have power to act in the name of the government. We takes prizes, and sells them, and that cripples our enemies, you see, while it makes us richer. But the main thing, miss, is to make sure them British don't try to make us into a colony again. No, sir, we're free, and we mean to remain our own men!"

Thoughtful, Diana helped him hold the sailor's leg steady as he bound the cloth about it. Suddenly she became aware of a dark shadow looming over her. The captain spoke.

"About done, Eli? I've finished the lot over there."

"Yes, sir, Captain. Just about done, thanks to the little lady, here. She be a fine one," said Eli cheerily.

The captain reached down, put his hands around Diana's slim waist, and lifted her to her feet. It was so simply done, and she was so quickly released, that she could not complain he was taking advantage of her. Yet the strong touch of his hands lingered, as though he held her still.

His eyes studied her gravely as she turned to face him. She was aware of her bloodied dress, her hair wildly mussed by the sea wind, her reddened hands, the weariness of her body, which she had held so rigidly, so as not to give in to the horror she felt at the sight of men's wounded bodies.

"We thank you, my lady," he said, in his calm voice. "Now, let me escort you to your cabin, and allow you some rest before dinner. We dine at seven, and will be pleased at your presence."

The ship rocked abruptly under her as a sharp wind rose. She staggered and gripped for the rail, but it was too far from her. The captain caught at her arm and held her easily against the lurch of the vessel. He urged her toward the brief flight of stairs down to her cabin.

He saw her inside, bowed courteously, and left her. The door closed. Hester started up from where she rested. "Oh, my lady, wherever have you been, and your father asking for you?" she asked anxiously, looking somewhat green.

"Lie down again, Hester. You are suffering again from the motion. I was on deck," she said with composure. She removed her gown and rinsed out the stains, over her maid's feeble objections. The woman looked quite ill from the excitement and danger.

Diana lay down on her bunk, recalling it was that of the captain. It was narrow, but comfortable. From there, she could see his desk, now barren of his possessions. A picture of a gallant ship, her white sails out in full rig, was the only ornament on the walls. She studied it as she lay there.

A clock somewhere chimed sweetly at six-thirty. Diana rose, surprised to find that she had slept, though lightly. Hester slept deeply. Diana bathed her face and got out a fresh dress. With a twitch of her lips, she found a gown she liked, the pink-and-silver-striped French taffeta. It was somewhat grand for aboard ship, but it was long-sleeved and high-necked, and would be warm against the cool night air.

She dressed, managing not to waken the maid, brushed out her long blonde hair, and styled it in curls as fashionable as though she were going to a ball. Wings swept back from either temple, in a simple design she liked. She studied her dark brown eyebrows, her vivid blue eyes, and found she needed no rouge for her cheeks; they were rosy from the wind.

Quietly, she left the cabin, then frowned. She did not know which way to turn. She had not paused long when a seaman darted forward from a perch near the entrance to her cabin.

The boy beamed at her, and directed her to the dining cabin. She entered, her chin up, to find the room empty. The little midshipman, glancing about, finally held out the chair to the right of the head. She thanked him, smiled, and sat down.

The door opened again, and in came Captain

McCullough. He smiled to see her, bowed courteously, and inquired after her health.

"I am quite well, I thank you, Captain. And may I thank you for the courtesy of your cabin? My maid and I are most comfortable."

His bronze-gold hair shone under the swinging lantern above the table. He bowed deeply, his eyes amused. "You are most welcome, my lady. May I offer you some sherry? From the West Indies, very fine stuff," he added, as she nodded.

He poured out the golden-brown liquor into small glasses which glittered in his hand. "Impressed from a British ship, sir?" she asked, accepting the glass.

"Ah, you understand us well! I am carrying it back to Boston where it might be more appreciated than in London, where they drink so much they do not taste any liquor!"

His mocking eyes dared her to match wits further with him. She only smiled, tasted the sherry and found it delicious.

"Your man, Mr. Ulrich," she said finally. "He seems most competent in medicine, as you are yourself, sir."

He leaned against the sideboard, which was securely fastened to the wall. "Ah, indeed, my lady. We must aye learn many trades for the sea. Eli has been with me many years. We are fast friends, as you will find."

The man he spoke of came in at that moment, attired in a fresh blue jacket, his hair brushed back. "Ah, my lady, I rejoice to see you at our table! Ain't seen many ladies these months, eh, Captain?"

Captain McCullough grinned. "You haven't, you old sea dog. Only barmaids at the taverns on the docks! I was more fortunate, having errands in London."

"Dammit, I must have my papers back!" Lord Hubert stormed into the cabin, his face flushed, his eyes bulging. "My valet tells me you stole my papers, Captain!"

His dark eyebrows were raised as the captain stared at Lord Hubert Somerville. "Stole? Such language, my lord. Must I remind you you are my prisoner?"

"Dammit, sir, I am on a peaceful trade mission to your country. This is beyond belief, that you should take my papers!"

"Peaceful? Your guns did not sound peaceful to me. Must be something wrong with my ears," said the captain, but his eyes were not amused, and his generous mouth had gone tight. Sir Geoffrey came in then to add his protests.

"My papers are missing, my entire diplomatic valise!" he said angrily. "Where are they? Are they still on the *Ulysses*? The valet swears he had them—"

Captain McCullough sighed. "Gentlemen, gentlemen, where is your comprehension? We are enemies, are we not? I have taken your papers to examine them."

"But I must have them back! Have you no sense

of honor?" wailed Lord Hubert, sounding more and more like a petulant child, his daughter thought coldly. "Where are they?"

"I have them safe, never fear. They shall be turned over to the authorities," said Captain McCullough. "Pray you be seated, and have some of this fine sherry. Dinner will be served as soon as Captain Talbot appears."

The British captain arrived at that moment, took in the red flushed faces of his compatriots, and Diana's serene air. Bemused, he took the chair held for him, at the end of the table opposite the American captain's chair.

"Captain Talbot," Lord Somerville turned to him. "You might try to get it through this man's head that I must have my diplomatic papers. He has no right to them. I am on a peaceful trade mission—"

"Pray be seated," Captain McCullough interrupted sternly. His hard look made them take chairs unwillingly, both across from Diana. Eli Ulrich took the seat on her right, and two other young officers came in quietly to join them.

Lord Somerville was about to speak again when the Yankee captain interrupted him.

"We will have grace," he said, and bowed his head. Diana at once bowed hers, stunned with surprise. With closed eyes, she heard his deep voice raised in prayer. "Oh, Lord God of the seas and the skies, we thank thee for yet another day of salvation. Thou hast preserved us yet again, and given us another victory, with no lives lost, thank

God! Bless this food to our use, and our bodies to thy service. In the name of the Blessed Jesus, we pray. Amen."

The others muttered *amen*, Diana among them. Her father seemed too shocked to speak. Grace had never been said at his own table, though he gave lip service to his church, and appointed the livings of the parishes in his jurisdiction with stern impartiality.

Diana was too moved to speak for a minute. This man had spoken so naturally, so fervently, she knew he meant every word he said. This had been no show for guests, no mockery. This sea captain believed firmly that God had been with him in the victory. He now motioned for the midshipman who hovered nearby to begin serving, and the boy brought a huge pot over to Diana.

Eli Ulrich leaned over to murmur encouragingly, "Boston baked brown beans, ma'am, a delicacy with us. You will enjoy it."

Diana smiled, took a generous serving, and tasted it. Her father watched with a suspicious frown. "Um—delicious," she said. "I must ask for the recipe."

Another midshipman brought a large platter of fish, and again she took some. Sir Geoffrey shuddered over the beans, and refused them, also her father. The Americans and the British captain helped themselves, and ate heartily. Finally a glass of wine served to calm Lord Somerville. He turned to Captain McCullough once again.

"Sir, I must ask you to return my diplomatic papers, and Sir Geoffrey's as well. They are of the utmost importance to us."

Captain McCullough eyed him calmly. "They will be safe with me," he said finally. "When we dock, I shall turn them over to the authorities. They may well return them to you. But we must examine them first, you must comprehend that."

"But dammit, we are not enemies! War has not been declared!" Lord Somerville grew red again.

"I beg you will not disturb yourself about it. The matter is closed," said Captain McCullough.

Sir Geoffrey seemed about to speak, then closed his mouth tightly. His light gray eyes were—as though he were planning something, Diana thought suspiciously. But what could he possibly plan? They were prisoners, as the captain had reminded them. It was only due to his courtesy that they sat at table with him, rather than in the hold, with chains on their ankles.

And Geoffrey had brought it on himself, she thought, feeling curiously vengeful. He *would* attack the Yankee brig, and think to impress their seamen! Now he found himself on that very ship, himself a prisoner.

By the serving of the delicious cold pudding as dessert, Lord Somerville's temper had improved, and his smooth manners reasserted themselves. He turned once again to McCullough.

"I must ask you earnestly, Captain McCullough," he said politely, "to turn about and return us to England."

"I do not know why I should," said Jeremy

McCullough, holding up a glass of golden wine and studying it in the light. "Excellent Spanish wine, sir; I commend it to you."

"Thank you. But you must see reason, sir. We must return to England. We are only a few days out; it will not put you amiss by many days. I shall make it worth your trouble."

"No, no, sir," and the captain laughed pleasantly. "You are bound for America, and to America you must go. And I am bound there myself. I have not been home these many months, and I long to see my family."

His family. He had not said he had a family, except sisters. Did he perhaps have a wife, in spite of his denial? His bright green gaze caught Diana's thoughtful stare. He smiled at her.

"This is your first trip to my country, my lady? I shall do my best to see that you enjoy it. Boston will be a surprise to you. The streets are handsomely laid out. The port is one of the finest. My father is a shipbuilder, and he will much enjoy showing you about our docks, and the new ships we are building."

"Thank you, Captain, you are most gracious," said Diana. "I am not sure what plans my father has. I must accompany him, of course."

"But, my lady," smiled the captain, his eyes devilish now, "you are *all* going with me—of course. How could it be otherwise?" And he flung back his head and laughed. Outside the wind roared and echoed the bluster of his laughter.

The light above the table caught the hard

planes of his tanned cheeks, and his shoulders moved arrogantly in the well-cut dark blue jacket. Diana remembered the hardness of his chest as she had struck him, the toughness of his arms as he had carried her like a child across the planks between the ships. The gilt buttons of his jacket were no brighter than his green eyes. This was a hard man, and a smart one, she thought. Her father would be wise to take warning. And so would she, thought Diana. So would she.

Chapter 6

The days passed pleasantly for Diana. The weather was warm for a time, and in her light muslins, with a cape drawn about her shoulders, she was warm enough on deck, and cool enough in the rather airless cabins.

She helped Eli Ulrich tend the wounded, going each day to the hold where they lay groaning in their bunks. Two men tended them constantly, but they always seemed glad to see Eli and Lady Diana approach with pots of salve, fresh bandages, and cool water.

Water had to be rationed. A seaman in the lookout scanned the skies for rain, but none came. So the water kegs could not be refilled, and the remaining water was used only for drinking. They washed in salt water, except the wounded.

The captain of the Yankee brig was ever gallant to Diana, and courteous to his British "guests," but he kept a sharp eye on them. Lord Hubert and Sir Geoffrey were not allowed up on his bridge, nor on deck when a sail was sighted in the distance. Only Diana and her maid had any degree of freedom about the ship, and even so a midshipman, a pleasant lad of about fourteen, tagged along behind her. She did not know if he watched her or guarded her, but he always greeted her with a shy smile when she emerged from the cabin.

He was Midshipman Fred Mullins, he had told her seriously, but she might call him "Fred," if she would. And she had gravely asked him to call her "Lady Diana," rather than the formal "my lady." Fred was from Maine, he explained when Diana commented on his accent, so different from the captain's. He was proud to have signed on with the captain, for Jeremy McCullough was known up and down the coast, said Fred, for his daring and the prizes he had captured. The McCulloughs had been in shipbuilding for two generations, and had always gone to sea, from early times.

Diana often felt uncomfortable with the captain, for he seemed always to watch her sharply with his mocking eyes. Her shyness took the form of coldness. She spoke only when she was spoken to, and felt as constrained as she had many evenings in her father's home, when her role as his hostess prevented her from engaging in spontaneous conversation or revealing her lively sense of the ridiculous.

Captain McCullough took her to task one evening, as she came early to dinner. She had been on deck most of the afternoon, enjoying the fresh, keen air, the bright sunshine of the mid-Atlantic, the whipping snap of the sails. She admired the barefoot sailors who climbed agilely onto the masts, the lookout who swayed in his little perch atop the tall mast as he looked out to sea in all directions.

Diana was no longer fashionably pale. Not only were her cheeks always rosy, but she even had acquired a slight golden hue from the sun. At least she had no freckles, she thought, as she examined her face in the mirror.

She had gone that evening to the small, neatly fitted dining room, and found herself the first one there. In her simple, greenish-blue muslin gown, she wandered about the room, gazing from the porthole, examining with curiosity the neat fittings of the sideboard, the cunning silver rings which held wine bottles firmly in place no matter how the ship rocked.

She started at the voice behind her. "Do you like our ship, my lady?"

It was the cool tone of Captain McCullough.

She felt a little shiver—was it resentment?—travel down her spine. She collected her composure and turned slowly to face him. "Indeed, sir, your brig is very handsome and nicely fitted. I was admiring the way these little rings are set into the wood."

He came over to stand close beside her, turning a bottle in the ring. "Thank you," he said, with an undercurrent of laughter in his tone. "We come to take things for granted on shipboard. You said this was your first journey? May it not be your last. You make a good sailor."

"You are most kind." She moved to her usual chair, hoping uneasily that someone would come in soon. He seemed to read her mind with uncanny accuracy.

"The gentlemen are on deck, looking at a school of fish going by. An unusual variety for these waters. They will join us presently. Some sherry for you, my lady?" He held the bottle poised, and at her nod, he poured some into the crystal stemmed glass.

He sat down beside her, at the head of the table, his own glass in his hand. "Your health, my lady!" He raised the glass to her. She responded with a brief nod, irritated anew. He was too courteous; she always suspected him when he was like this.

Captain McCullough looked at her over his glass, his eyes mischievous. "My lady," he said in a lower tone, "until I met you, I thought no one could be so cool, so composed. Any other woman would have screamed or fallen into a faint at the sight we—ah—made that evening."

"I regret so much to have disappointed you," she said in an icy tone. She sipped the sherry. It was indeed excellent.

"I was not at all disappointed; intrigued rather. When you confessed that the unconscious gentleman was your fiancé, and you showed not the slightest sign of discomposure, I was moved to wonder what had caused your engagement. Your father, perhaps? It was his match?"

She stared into space, painfully aware of his gaze on her. "It is not your concern, Captain."

"You would be amazed, my lady—" He caught himself. "All on board ship is my concern, Lady

Diana. The—ah—closeness of your relationship to Sir Geoffrey is of concern."

"I cannot imagine why."

He half-smiled. She caught the movement of his golden head as he lifted it under the lamplight. "Your marriage was arranged, I believe. But you and your fiancé are equally cold to it. Why not break it off?"

She was startled into turning her head to meet his narrowed gaze. "Sir, you are impertinent!"

"Not at all. Merely—inquisitive. Arranged marriages are not quite the thing in the—ah—former colonies, you know. Love matches are quite the style now, as much in style as your bonnet. I thought you should know," he added gently, "before you visit our shores. Else you might wonder at the devotion between husband and wife that you will find there."

"Do you mean to say there are no arranged marriages—" She was disturbed at her own interest, the quickening of her heartbeat. She set down her glass carefully, so the trembling of her hand would not show. Yet she felt somehow he had noticed this also.

"Not at all. There are some, among the very wealthy. But most of us do our own courting. You know, I have the impression, my lady, that you have never been courted. You should be, you know. It would warm your cold heart, melt your hard pride."

She bit her lip, aware of a desire to slap him. He laughed softly, as if he understood that, too.

"You might be interested in the courting customs of the Americans," the cool mocking tone went on in her burning ear. "A man will come to the home of his sweetheart, and on a cold night, they go to bed together."

"Sir!"

"It is true. The mother will place them in bed herself, with a long bolster pillow between them, and they will talk, laugh, read together, the entire evening, with no thought of intimacy. It is a custom called bundling. I recommend it," he added, lifting his glass and draining it.

She shifted uneasily, sure he was teasing her with some untruth. "I find it hard to believe well-brought-up females do this," she said stiffly.

"Ask my sisters when you meet them," he replied at once. "Oh, and there are other customs. Some couples meet at church, and attend choir together of an evening. They walk together in the starlight and talk of what they will. They are not chaperoned everywhere. The eldest of my three sisters is walking out with a young man from the ship firm my father owns. He is a good man, the family approves of him. But should she marry him, 'twill be her choice, not one imposed by our father."

She gazed down at her plate and was relieved when the door opened and her father came in. He cast a keen, troubled look at his daughter, noting her flushed cheeks, the sparkle in her blue eyes. Then he looked toward the captain, who appeared as unruffled as always. "Diana, you should have come on deck with us."

"I was on deck earlier, Papa," she said quietly. "The wind was rising, and I finally went below to my cabin. You have enjoyed the day, I hope?"

Her tone was as measured as usual. Lord Hubert accepted the glass of sherry and sat down with relief. He must have imagined some tension between them, yet he resolved not to leave them alone. Diana was uneasy with Sir Geoffrey, and that worthy gentleman was too cool to Diana as well. There might be trouble before the bonds were safely tied.

"What were you discussing when I entered?" asked Lord Somerville with pretended casualness.

"Some customs of the Americans," Captain McCullough answered for her. "I am anxious that all of you find yourselves at home in my country, and take interest in all that goes on. Lady Diana will, of course, meet my sisters, and other young ladies. Their freedom of movement might be strange and shocking to her. Yet they are modest and demure in our own lights."

"Of course, of course," murmured Lord Somerville. Captain Talbot came in, followed by the others. Sir Geoffrey seemed distracted, and Lord Somerville sighed a little, wishing he could give the man a good shaking. Diana was rather like her mother; she might be brooding over the lack of attentions from her fiancé. All females seemed to like attention, the more the better.

After dinner, Diana excused herself and went to

her cabin. But it was stiflingly warm in spite of the open porthole, and she finally took her wool cloak and went on deck, into the starlit night.

The little midshipman followed her. She smiled down at him, and he beamed at her shyly, and leaned on the rail beside her.

"Do you know, the stars are all in certain places in the sky?" he told her.

"Indeed? Tell me about it, Fred."

He pointed out some of the constellations proudly and drew her gaze to the North Star, "which is what we steer by, Lady Diana," he said. "It is like the star in one's life, a goal toward which one must steer if one is not to go astray."

She thought about that in silence. How wise a boy he was. He yawned widely, and she finally said, "You must go below and get your sleep, Fred. Are you on watch tonight?"

He had confided that he stood watch some nights. He nodded. "Yes, my lady."

"Then go and get some sleep first," she urged gently. "I shall go below shortly."

He finally left her reluctantly, and another shadow detached itself from those behind her, and came to the rail. "You enjoy the stars, my lady?"

"Yes, indeed, Captain, but I must go below," she said stiffly, making to turn about.

His voice had startled her. She wondered how long he had stood behind them, listening to their conversation. He moved as silently as a great tawny cat at times.

She clung to the rail as the ship slanted to one

side, then back to the other side, to come erect again.

"We shall have a storm in a day or two," he said easily. "The water is swelling beneath us, and the skies to the west are gathering clouds."

"Did you tell the lad about the North Star and steering toward a goal in life?" she asked abruptly.

He moved closer, to lean on the rail, his arm close to hers. "Aye, yes, I talk to my lads," he said gently. "Some come from farms, and know naught but the land. Others are from closemouthed families, and their fathers had naught to say to them of life. I but tell them what I would say to my own sons."

"You have sons?"

He laughed softly. "I told you, no, I have no wife. No family but my parents, three sisters, and three brothers. You will meet them in Boston," he added confidently.

She felt immensely relieved, then angry with herself for feeling so. But she could picture him with sons of his own, of the same tawny-gold hair, the laughing recklessness, the golden tan of their youthful cheeks promising to turn to his own dark tan.

"Howard is the eldest," went on Jeremy McCullough, as she did not speak then. "He has a mathematical turn of mind, and is of much assistance to my father in the shipyards. He and Anthony are both married to fine girls, and setting up homes of their own. Anthony is studying law. Then there is Angela. She is eighteen, and walking out. Then Teresa, and Donald, and Penelope."

"Such a big family," she murmured wistfully. He spoke of them with such warmth. "How does your mother manage?"

He smiled. "You may well ask. *She* does sometimes, when she is maddened by us. But she will set everyone to work, and order us about, until all is right again. And what of you? You have lost your mother, I believe?"

Responding to the gentleness of his tone, she nodded. "Yes, Mother died when I was ten. I have been alone since then— I mean—there is but my brother Thomas, who has set up on his own. He is twenty-six. And Father— I am his hostess."

"And a cold fish to boot," murmured the reckless voice in her ear. "Does he try to model you in his fashion? Yes, I can see that he tries. But you have warmth in you, under that ice."

She stiffened and drew away from him. "Sir, you are impertinent again!"

"It is my nature," he laughed softly. "What did they do to you, Lady Diana? When your mother died, did all warmth die with her? Do you do your duty, as you are told, and think no more of it?"

Speaking of her mother brought tears to her eyes; the waves of the dark blue ocean were a blur. She composed her tone to coolness once again. "I have always tried to do my duty, sir."

"I am sure of it. You are encased in it!" Then his voice changed. "Why—you are weeping. There goes a diamond tear down your soft cheek." His hand came up, flicked gently at the tear that was coursing its way down her cheek. "I'm sorry, it was too bad of me. Don't weep."

His arms went about her, drawing her to him, as though she were a child to be comforted. She drew a trembling breath and fought back the tears. She rarely cried, and then alone in her bedroom. But his arms were so warm and comforting, and when he pressed her face against the scratchy wool of his jacket, she longed to rub her cheek against it.

He ran his hand down over her back in a gentle manner. She felt a strange thrill going through her, like the thrill when he had waltzed with her in Prince Alexei's ballroom. She began to draw back. His hand went to her hair, softly drawn back in a chignon for coolness, revealing the purity of the lines of her face. His fingers caressed her hair, moved down to her neck.

His arms tightened as she moved against him. The grip on her changed, from that of a man holding a hurt child to that of a man who felt the softness of a woman in his arms. He pulled her hard against him, and his hand went down to the curve of her back. He drew her so closely against him she felt as though she were one with him.

"Diana, Diana," he whispered, and with his other hand he turned her face toward his imperiously. He searched her face in the starlight, his gaze keen even in the darkness. She was aware of the warmth emanating from him, the hardness of the grip in which she was held. Yet she could not struggle, caught as she was in a silken net. Unable to move, to sigh, to protest.

His hard mouth came down on hers. Once again he kissed her, but not hastily this time. His mouth lingered, moved to her cheek, then back hotly to her lips again. He forced her lips open, and his mouth was demanding on hers. Demanding. He wanted passion from her— And his passion was hot and sweet.

The shock of it made her go limp, and for a long moment she yielded, her slim body swayed into his hardness, her hands clutching at his wide shoulders. She was aware of the night, the shadows, the heat of his body on hers, the warmth of his mouth, the response beginning to well up in her, the softness in the core of her that wanted to linger, to be commanded, to be overcome.

"Diana! Is that you!" Sir Geoffrey's voice was coldly astonished. "Diana? Diana? What the devil are you doing, sir?" he demanded.

Captain McCullough slowly let her go. Diana fell back against the hard railing, feeling as though her knees would scarcely hold her up. She stared through the darkness at the face of her fiancé.

"What the devil— How dare you, sir! You are taking advantage of your position!" Sir Geoffrey was wildly angry. He had hated his position as a prisoner, he had resented daily and nightly their place on this ship, the failure of his attack on the inferior brig. And now this Yankee captain was holding his fiancée, *kissing* her!

He struck out at Jeremy McCullough. The man easily fended him off and gave a sharp order. "Carter! Prentice!" Two sailors appeared at once.

"You'll see Sir Geoffrey to his cabin," said the captain, every inch in command now.

"How dare you?" cried Sir Geoffrey. "You attacked my fiancée!"

"I did not attack her. I kissed her," said Jeremy, laughter in his tone. "I think she has not had much of kissing. Americans do not linger so long over their courting, nor over their fighting!"

Geoffrey reached instinctively for the sword that was not at his side. "Name your seconds, sir!"

"Nonsense," said the captain. "Go below. Lock him in his cabin until he cools off."

Diana covered her face with her hands. She felt bitterly ashamed, that two men had come to blows over her, that her fiancé had seen her in another man's embrace, lost to all caution. She, the cool, the chaste. . . .

Geoffrey yelled back at them as he was dragged away: "I will fight you, Captain! You will not evade me! You have defiled my fiancée! You will be sorry for this—"

Diana straightened her shoulders. "I would go below," she said coldly, to cover her fright and shame.

Jeremy put his hand on her shoulder. She shuddered, afraid of him suddenly. Did he mean to have her? He was captain, solely in command here. He could rape her, and none could stop him. And she occupied his cabin!

"Do not worry, Diana," he said gently. "We shall have you out of this coil. I do not intend—"

"Diana? Is that you, child? Whatever has happened to Geoffrey?" Lord Hubert stumbled onto the deck, gazing about in bewilderment as Diana came forward, her arm in Captain McCullough's grip. "What is this? Has this man attacked you?"

His distraught face was greenish in the light of a torch flaming in the hands of a sailor who stood watchfully beside him.

"It is nothing, Father," she said, but her voice shook. "Sir Geoffrey—misunderstood. I am going below now."

Captain McCullough stepped back as she took her father's arm. "I will say good night now, Lady Diana. Sleep well, and do not fret about this." And he turned and walked away into the shadows.

Lord Somerville escorted his daughter to her cabin. He stared keenly at her pale face. She looked upset, her hair mussed, her cloak half off her shoulders. Had that man dared—

"Lord, Lord, here is a turmoil," he said more quietly. "As though we were not in enough trouble. *Did* the man attack you?"

"No, Father. He—he kissed me. That is all." She took off her cloak, and Hester accepted it from her. Her hands were trembling; she longed to be alone to think, to feel—no, she must not feel. This was wrong, wrong.

"Kissed you?" Lord Somerville strode back and forth in agitation. His daughter looked too much like her mother tonight, her mouth quivering and scarlet, her blue eyes shining with tears. It recalled unpleasant scenes, when his wife had accused him of coldness, of liking his work more than herself. Quarrels had followed, in which he had insisted on having his way. She must leave the child and come to a ball with him; he could not remain at home because an important meeting was taking place; the governess could look after Diana when she was ill, his wife must come to London with him. He had won, but he had had an uneasy feeling that these were empty victories, for his wife had turned cool to him.

If Diana was going to act like her mother, she could not have chosen a worse time to do so. There would be diplomatic repercussions enough from the loss of the *Ulysses*, their arrival in Boston as prisoners rather than as diplomats. Sir Geoffrey had acted foolishly in urging the attack on the Yankee brig, for they had lost. And now if he were to lose his fiancée to this brash Yankee, if Diana lost her innocence to that captain, all hell would break loose. Diana was not a female to lose her virtue without a fight, he felt sure. And Sir Geoffrey would not accept her as a bride without her virtue. Damn it all! The Prince Regent would hear of it—a distant relative losing his fiancée in this outlandish manner. Lord Hubert ran a distracted hand through his hair, and realized he had forgotten his wig.

He would be happy to land. This was a dreadful voyage, an unlucky voyage, though usually he was not one to believe in luck. But all had gone wrong from the night of the ball when the Russian's papers had been taken, the night he had first learned of the dangerous American who now . . . He looked at Diana with exasperation and some dislike. That was what came of taking females along. Something went wrong. No wonder many seamen would not permit females on board ship. He said good night to her brusquely, and went below to his own cabin.

Diana closed the door after him in great relief. If she could only close out her thoughts and emotions so easily! She permitted herself to be undressed, dutifully put on a thin chiffon gown of blue, then sat down to have her hair brushed out.

In the mirror, she saw Hester's worried face. But the woman was silent, perhaps in sympathy. She closed her eyes, and thought of the strength of Jeremy's embrace, the heat of his mouth, the urgency of his lips against hers. As though he wanted her badly.

She compared it with the cool, wet touch of Sir Geoffrey's mouth on her cheek, the few times she had permitted it. She swallowed. She must forget—she must forget— She was promised to Sir Geoffrey. He was a close friend of the Prince Regent, and a distant relative of his. Her father's career must not be impeded by her own rash behavior. The marriage must go through, even if she and Sir Geoffrey came to dislike each other intensely.

But even as she lay wide-eyed in her bunk later on, and tried in vain to woo sleep, she could not help thinking of Jeremy and his kisses, and the way he had described marriage among the Americans, how they chose their own partners for life, how happy they were. She stuffed her fist into her mouth to keep back the sobs that might disturb her maid. That way was not for her. She was British, and she had a duty to perform. That was the way she had been raised.

Chapter 7

Diana slept uneasily, and finally fell into a heavy sleep toward dawn. She wakened late, to the thud of bare feet on the stairs and on the deck above. As she turned over in the bunk, her head aching, she heard the sharp smack of bullets as the sailors began gunnery practice.

She lay there for a time. Hester sat near the window, working on her embroidery, waiting for her mistress to rouse. Diana did not want to wake up.

She knew she could have prevented that embrace last night. No wonder the Yankee captain held her so cheap. No wonder her father was upset. She spared a dispassionate thought for Sir Geoffrey, locked in his cabin. He would be angry with her, but she could not bring herself to care. She did care what Jeremy McCullough thought of her, though. She did not wish him to think her a cheap woman.

She folded her arms behind her head and listened to the sharp commands above her, the guns replying. Finally it ceased, and heavy thuds and laughing voices told her the sailors had been dismissed to their usual duties.

Captain Talbot had expressed his amazement that gunnery practice was carried on daily on the

Yankee brig. Captain McCullough had told him casually that it helped improve their marksmanship. He gave prizes for the best marks, and at the end of the voyage, they had a grand competition.

"Furthermore, when we are in battle, they have a better eye for the targets, as you have witnessed," said McCullough, a gleam in his eyes.

Captain Talbot flushed but nodded in agreement. "We should practice more, but our men are often from the city streets, and know nothing of rifles and pistols. The farm lads sometimes are better at that, but turn green at the rolling of the ship."

"That is what comes of impressing men, rather than enlisting them for pay," said McCullough, and then cooled the hot argument that followed with a few crisp orders directed at his men.

He could be a devil at times, thought Diana now, turning over to sit up.

"You are awake, my lady?" asked Hester softly, concern in her eyes as she rose.

"Yes, yes. What kind of day is it?"

"A gray one, my lady. Looks as though we may get a storm," and the maid gulped uneasily. "Do you think it might be bad? Have any said aught?"

"They hope for rain to fill the water barrels," said Diana, sliding from the warm bed with a sigh. She did not want to face this day. She hated her own cowardice, but how could she look the Yankee captain in the face? He must have sensed her yielding.

She bathed briefly in the cool salt water of the

basin, then dressed in a dark blue gown of practical serge. She fastened her hair back in a braid, then wound it round her head. Her face was pale from lack of sleep, and there were dark shadows like bruises under her eyes. She turned from the small mirror with a shrug. What did it matter how she looked?

Fred brought a tray to the cabin, and she drank tea, and ate a little bread. Then she went below to join Eli Ulrich in the hold, where he was tending the wounded. He looked up with a grin, and a keen gaze at her face.

"There you are, my lady. I wondered if I should have my assistant today," he said jovially.

She managed to smile at him, and at the British lad he tended. She knelt beside the bunk to assist in the bandaging, but she was very quiet, speaking little as they tended the men.

The one with the lost arm was feverish today, and Eli looked grave over him. He did not seem to know them, but tossed and turned, and had to be tied to his bunk.

"I'll be glad when we get to Boston, where he can have a proper surgeon," said Eli, when they had finished. He escorted her to her cabin, where she washed her hands and arms in the salt water to guard against infection. "You'll come out on deck, my lady? You need a bit of fresh air."

She was glad to go with the kindly first mate. He was thoughtful and considerate to her, as her father had never been.

Captain McCullough stood near the wheel, talk-

ing to two of his men in an absorbed way. He
looked up briefly when Diana and Eli appeared,
flung them a crisp salute, then turned to the sailors again.

Eli led Diana to another part of the deck, and
they leaned against the railing, a companionable
silence stretching between them.

"You heard of—last night?" she finally ventured
unhappily.

"Yes, Lady Diana. Now, you're not to fret about
it. Your fiancé will be released shortly. It ain't the
captain's way to take offense. Ain't worried about
their dueling, are you?"

She bit her lip. She was ashamed to admit that
was the least of her worries. She had wondered if
the captain thought her a loose woman, his for the
taking. She merely shook her head and turned her
face away.

"Ah, well, none of you knows the captain like I
does," said Eli cheerily. "Did I tell you of the time
when he and me first went to sea, and him green
as grass?"

"No, I don't think so."

"Well, here was I, in my mid-thirties, with a
family grown. And here was this young sprig, son
of the boss, and a grand man by his clothes. And
he comes to me, and says as how he wants to learn
everything."

The shrewd eyes looked sideways at her for encouragement. She looked to him eagerly. "Oh,
yes—what did you say?"

He needed no more. "Well now, I says, do you

want to know everything today, or should we keep a couple facts against tomorrow when it might be dull?"

They both laughed, and Diana felt a little easier.

"Well, that day," said Eli, settling himself comfortably against the railing, "comes up a storm, and I mean a good, solid, gray sou'wester. The wind, she howled like a lost soul, and the rain poured down. And there was young sprig out in it, his coat off, his shirt soaking wet, hauling out rain barrels to catch the rain. I helps him, of course, and we catch a good haul. Then he's looking about, and I says, what is it you're alooking fer?"

Her blue eyes sparkled as she listened, picturing the scene.

"More barrels," said Eli impressively. "I tells him, 'We filled every cussed barrel on this ship, and if you think I'm staying out here and getting colder, you got another think coming!' And I go down to mess, and get myself a hot toddy with rum to the brim. So down he comes, rubbing himself with a towel, looks at me, and helps himself to the rum. So we got drunk together, and sung many a song the rest of the night!"

She laughed softly at the warm picture he had made. What a comradeship was that of the sea.

The man went on, eager at her appreciation.

"Well, now we was sailing down to the south, to the Indies. And right off, what do we see but a treasure ship. We knows it's loaded, for she's down to the waterline with her haul, and coming out of Jamaica, bound for England. Young sprig, he sees her from up on the mast, and calls out. Captain wants to know if we can take her. How big is she? Young sprig says, easy. And so up we come with a gray flag on us until we sees what flag the stranger carries. And then we both put out our flags, us the American flag, and the other a British flag. But how the captain cussed when he sees she has nigh on forty guns, and us with but twenty!"

The blue eyes widened at him. "Oh, what happened then?"

"Why, we attacked, of course," said Eli ruefully. "We shift into the wind, and with the wind at our backs, we run down her side, and give her a cannonade. And young sprig up in the mast, howling for more ammunition and a hardy lad to help him. So I'm so stupid I go up the mast with him, and we have ourselves a time, shooting down into the very deck of the other ship."

"And then what happened?"

"We captures her," said Eli, censoring part of his story for her delicate ears. "And then we open up the hold, and what do you think—cases of fine rum! And jewels from Brazil and them parts, emeralds and diamonds like I never seen in my life."

He held her enthralled by his stories, which went on and on. He told of capturing other ships, how Jeremy had learned and trained, and finally had been given his own ship. He had asked Eli to come and serve with him.

"With him, mind you, my lady," said Eli

proudly. "That's the way the captain is. He asks for volunteers to serve with him. Every lad on board is one he chose himself, and many could wish to come, but he won't have a brute, nor a bad 'un with him. He picks and chooses, and many more would come if there was room. And always he gets the prizes, and hauls them home, like a young lad showing off to his mother what he gets for her, silks, and taffetys, and jewels for the mum and his sisters, and rum for his father and fat cigars from Cuba—" Eli shook his head.

Diana found herself smiling at the picture of that self-assured man of the world, bringing back prizes to his mother and sisters. What a man, with a boy yet inside him. That accounted for his sunny laughter, the sparkle in his eyes, the gaiety that nothing could quash.

Eli went on: "There was the time we captures a load of women. My, the lads were going on about what fun they would have. But the captain, he tells them how skeered the females are, and how they have families at home, and young'uns, too, and we must be nice and pleasant to them. Well, we was, too, escorting them home to France, and letting them off in some port, with the captain hiring carriages to take them home. Reckon some of them ladies wouldn't ha' minded staying with the captain, but he ain't the sort."

Diana turned thoughtful, gazing out at the darkening sea and the western sky where gray clouds were gathering. "Do you mean—he is not a ladies' man?"

"Well, now, he's all for the dancing and party-
ing when the work is done, my lady," said Eli, with
a grin. "But he ain't one to bring a female aboard,
as many of 'em does."

A familiar voice made her start, as the captain
came up behind them. "Eli, you have talked long
enough. Have you told her every wild sea story
that you know?" And he came to lean against the
railing and survey her flushed cheeks.

"Just about," said Eli, with a wink at Diana.
"Ain't told her about the mermaids yet, though.
I'll save that one for later!" And with a laugh, he
strolled away.

"Are—are we going to have a storm, Captain?"
she asked nervously.

"Looks like. We can use the rain. Enjoy the air
while you can, Lady Diana," he said pleasantly.
"You may have to remain in your cabin during the
storm. They can sweep a body overboard, and I
have vowed to protect you, after all."

She gazed up at him, her blue eyes darkened
with worry. He smiled down at her brilliantly and
pressed her slim hand that gripped the railing.
"Still worried?" he mocked gently. "You need
have no worries aboard my ship, I assure you."

Somehow he must have sensed her fears about
his attacking her. She flushed hotly, and her gaze
dropped. He gave her hand a final reassuring
squeeze, then released it.

"Stay out as long as you desire. I'll send Fred to
tell you should it be dangerous on deck, my lady,"

he said briskly, then touched his cocked black hat and left her to muse there.

She watched the darkening sky for a time, strangely at ease once again. The ship stirred under her feet, as though aware of the growing storm. By the time she went down for luncheon, the *Eagle* was tossing on a series of deeper waves and troughs.

The plates on the table were set today inside small metal circles, cunningly attached to the beautiful boards. The wine glasses were set in smaller metal rings. The midshipman swayed as he moved carefully from one person to another with the hot dishes.

The captain did not come down, nor did Sir Geoffrey. Eli Ulrich murmured something about the Englishman's remaining in his cabin. Finally, toward the end of the meal, the captain appeared, his head bare, his tawny-gold hair tossed by the wind. He apologized briefly, and attacked his meal with appetite.

"Is Sir Geoffrey under detention yet today?" asked Lord Somerville pugnaciously.

Captain McCullough raised his dark eyebrows. "Until he cools down," he said cheerfully. "I do not think you would enjoy his language. I told him I would let him out when he can behave like a gentleman."

Lady Diana swallowed a hysterical giggle, giving her intent interest to the caramel custard before her. The captain continued to spoon up his food hungrily.

Lord Somerville reddened angrily. "He *is* a gentleman, Captain! I understand you refused to duel him."

Eli Ulrich caught his breath. The captain took a sip of wine and gazed thoughtfully at the British lord. "Indeed. I despise dueling," he said, with a ring to his voice that made Diana jump. "A cowardly, wasteful custom. We do not care for it in America!"

"Indeed! There are no gentlemen there either, I believe," sneered Lord Somerville.

"No, sir, no gentlemen, no titles. We are all equal under God, and hope to remain so, my lord! None shall own us or rule us, none but our chosen leaders by fair election!" In a calmer tone, he continued: "Also, I am captain of this brig. I shall not fight any but other ships while aboard her. However, if Sir Geoffrey wishes to fight me—with fists—I shall be glad to give him a chance at a dust-up once we are on land again." And he resumed his meal calmly, thanking the midshipman with a smile for the plate of fish set before him.

"Fight with fists!" said Lord Somerville in disgust. "That is not his way."

Diana thought again of the scene in Prince Alexei Troubetzkoy's study, when Sir Geoffrey had been knocked out by the Yankee captain. Once more she stared at her plate to refrain from laughing. What was the matter with her?

She should be sympathetic to Geoffrey, yet she found herself thinking of a strange land, where no duels were employed between "gentlemen." She knew such fights usually involved bored rakes with nothing to amuse themselves but the favors of a woman who was scarely worth a drop of their blood.

Freedom, their own men. Men with chins lifted high, not afraid to walk the streets of their cities for fear of impressment. Not bending the knee to a lord of the manor, nor groveling for favors that only the lord could grant, if he so chose.

Captain McCullough changed the conversation abruptly, and Diana felt a mixture of disappointment and relief.

By the end of the uneasy meal, the ship was lurching from side to side. The captain excused himself hastily and went up on deck again.

Eli Ulrich said, "You might go up for a short time, my lady, and see the sky as we approach the storm. It's a sight to behold. There's plenty of time before you have to go to your cabin."

She thanked him with a smile, and took his suggestion. She had come to value her time on deck, when she could lean on the rail, and watch the barefoot sailors dashing about gracefully, and climbing up the lean masts as nimbly as boys in an apple orchard. But she had to admit to herself that she watched eagerly for the Yankee captain, moving commandingly about the deck, pausing for a serious word or a shout of laughter with his men. He seemed a favorite with them; they treated him with more than respect—with a sort of devotion she had not seen before.

Diana went up on deck, a wool cloak wrapped

about her, a plain bonnet tied about her hair. The wind was much stronger now, and she felt a fine mist tingle against her cheeks.

The dark clouds were much closer, whipped on by the wind until they covered the western sky. She noted that some of the sails had been rolled up, and tied fast with ropes. The ship lurched deeply from side to side, then recovered her balance. Diana watched with keen interest, and only the smallest twinge of fear, as the dark clouds came closer. Presently all the sky seemed covered with their turbulence, and midday was almost as dark as noon. Eli Ulrich came up to her.

"You'd best go below, my lady, she'll be blowing stronger than this before long." He grinned at her. She let go the railing, stumbled, and he caught her arm in his strong grip and assisted her to the stairs. She was laughing as she practically fell down the short stairway to the door of her cabin. She felt strangely alive, full of excitement.

The cabin windows had been shut, and the little cabin was stifling hot. Diana removed her cloak, then her warm dress, and put on a thin silk gown of pale blue. Her hair had been flattened by the bonnet, and she brushed it out and fastened it back with a blue ribbon, simply, like a child's. Hester helped her, lurching about the cabin, her face greenish, until Diana begged her to lie down.

She had just done so when a brief tattoo sounded at the wooden door. Diana opened the door to find Jeremy McCullough grinning down at her. He was without his jacket, and his thin shirt was wet through, his hair dark with the dampness. He wore no shoes or boots, and his dark blue trousers had been rolled up to the knees. His eyes sparkled with animation.

"Pardon me, Lady Diana. I'll just make sure your windows are shut tight," he said cheerfully, and beckoned to the burly seaman behind him, who moved rapidly to check the windows. Captain McCullough glanced about critically.

"Best put all your gear into the valises, and tie them into the wardrobe," he said brusquely. "Should we roll about, and I think we will, you'll find them spilling over the floor, and maybe breaking. Stay inside. We'll be closing the hatches so water can't come through to the cabins below. Someone will bring some food to you when you're hungry. We dispense with formality during a storm."

She thanked him, he grinned again, and the two departed. Men, she thought. He looked as though he were enjoying the prospect of the storm. He must like fighting the elements. He certainly enjoyed dangers! But then Diana had to admit to herself that she, too, had been roused by the sight of the darkening sea and sky.

She took his advice, put her powder boxes, rouge pots, brushes, and mirrors into the valises, and stuffed everything into the wardrobe. She found a small cord to tie the door shut. Already the ship was rocking, and Hester moaning with every roll.

Diana seated herself on the bunk, with her back

to the headrest, and prepared to wait out the storm. The rain lashed against the windows, but they were closed tight. Not even a trickle of water seeped through. Not so the door; every now and then a roll of the ship brought water under it. She heard it sloshing about on the deck, and sometimes the call of a sailor for assistance.

The hours seemed to pass with agonizing slowness. She wondered how her father and Geoffrey endured it. Perhaps her fiancé was still locked in his cabin.

It was late afternoon when Fred brought a tray with a huge teapot, two cups of sturdy pewter, and a plate of sandwiches. She ate hungrily, but Hester could touch nothing but a little tea.

"Is it going to be a long storm?" Diana asked Fred.

"Oh, yes, mum, all the night, the captain says," he replied cheerfully. "The water kegs be filled already! It be a foot deep on deck at times! I almost washed overboard, but the captain, he grabbed me!"

The night passed slowly. Diana slept a little, and Hester finally dozed. Morning came with the sky still darkened, but the rain squalls seemed to have passed over. A seaman came to unfasten the windows, and fresh, sweet air filled the cabin.

Diana staggered about to wash and dress. She managed to climb up to the deck, where she stared about, amazed. The deck was washed clean by the storm. One mast hung broken, and the sails were still furled except for two large ones. The ship was traveling at a great rate toward the west now.

The captain came toward her, his eyes underscored with dark shadows, his chin covered with golden stubble. "Good morning, my lady. I trust you slept well?"

"As well as your storm would allow," she said with a smile. "I think you did not sleep?"

"No, my lady. Not while she's blowing like that," he said simply. "I wish you could have seen her buck the waves! She's a sweet, sturdy ship, well-built and trim."

So might he have described a sweetheart, thought Diana involuntarily, as she gazed beyond his keen eyes to the ship, and the seamen climbing up the mast to let out fresh sail. The huge white sails billowed out, and the ship seemed to shudder and run before the wind like a live thing. It was an indescribable sensation for her, like reaching freedom and air after the confinement of a prison cell.

"Captain McCullough! You are my prisoner now!" The strange cry came from Sir Geoffrey. Diana whirled around to see her fiancé standing, gaunt and unshaven, with a pistol pointed at Captain McCullough. Behind Sir Geoffrey stood a dozen of the British seamen, looking sullen and uneasy, with rifles and pistols in their hands.

Captain Talbot came up behind them, a cutlass raised in his big hands. Jeremy McCullough seemed to freeze where he stood.

Diana stepped quickly away from him, not wanting to hamper his movements.

"Indeed? I made a mistake in letting you free of your cabin during the storm," said McCullough dryly. His green eyes glittered.

"You made a mistake when you attacked us." Sir Geoffrey snarled at him. "Did you really think to keep me prisoner? I am a British subject, you a rebel. Come along, men, take over the ship."

"You would make a mistake to try it, Sir Geoffrey," said McCullough, almost gently.

The pistol raised, and Diana cried out. But when the trigger snapped, nothing happened. Sir Geoffrey looked down at the pistol in a daze.

"Look up," said McCullough. "My men in the rigging, sir!"

Diana raised her head. Up in the rigging, the men had drawn their pistols, and held them steadily on the British seamen on deck.

"Did you really believe," said McCullough softly, "that I would be fool enough to allow you to wander among your men, encouraging mutiny? You were overheard time and again. I left you in peace, to plan your plotting. But I think you had best be confined to cabin again!"

"You will never take me prisoner!" cried Sir Geoffrey, and he struggled against the firm grip of McCullough.

"Give it up, man," said McCullough, easily holding the man his own height, but not his strength. "Eli, call all the men on deck, all that can be spared, except the wounded."

"Aye, aye, sir!" And Eli Ulrich piped for the men. They came running up, to stand gaping at the British seamen.

"They have but empty pistols and no powder," said McCullough calmly. "I filled their powder horns with another powder—of the flour variety!"

A great gust of laughter went up from the American seamen. The British flung their pistols to the ground in disgust. An American went about collecting them, then stood back.

McCullough stood easily facing them then. His eyes blazed at the men who had rebelled against him, and tried to bring about a mutiny on his ship.

"Men, I will tell you once, and you will believe me," his strong voice rang across the deck, "that what Sir Geoffrey Loring told you was a lie! I do not impress you! When we reach America, you shall be given passage back to England, and to your homes, if you so desire!"

A young second lieutenant stepped forward and spoke into the silence following those words. "He said—sir—that you would force us to serve on American ships, and fight against our own! Or we would be placed in cells, to die!"

McCullough placed his hands on his hips. "I do not operate that way," he said calmly. He lifted his chin, square and stubborn. "Ask my men if I lie. No, whoever wishes to return to England shall have safe passage back there, to your homes, to your wives and sweethearts. But hear me!"

He paused, waiting for the uneasy stir to subside.

"Hear me!" The ringing voice went on. "I live in a free country, a wide and wild country. Beyond Boston lies the wilderness. A man may travel out to Ohio country, and farmland which will then belong to him. He may start a shop, and ask no man's leave. He may walk the streets freely, and not fear to be impressed and forced to serve for years on a ship. If he sails with me, he receives fair treatment, prize money, food to his liking, and rum as he wishes. America is the new land! There free men may live in a free country! Their freedom may not be taken from them by the whim of some—nobleman!" His gaze traveled scornfully over Sir Geoffrey.

The Britishers stirred, whispered, then settled to silence again. McCullough went on. Diana found herself listening as intently as the sailors, thrilling to his forceful words.

"My people fought a revolution against the mother country, because of unfair taxation, unfair trade practices, unfair treatment of her own citizens in America. We won that revolution, against all odds. We do not sit tamely while England tries to rule us again! Still England tries to blockade our ports, dictate trade to us. Her Parliament makes laws that impede us, as though with our permission. We have our own legislature, and our own president, to make the laws, and enforce them, *with* our permission! With our permission!"

He paused again, to let the words sink in. His gaze swept over them; his face was grave but his eyes aglow.

"For years the British impressed our citizens, on the pretext that they were British. We are not British! We are Americans! We are free men, and no man dictates to me what I shall do. I choose the men who will serve on my ship from those who come to me and ask to serve. The British force men to serve for many years away from their homes, be they farmers, or shop workers, or sheepherders! You will not find it so in my country!" His voice rang out proudly. "No, in America you will be free! I say again, if any man wishes to return home to England, he shall do so! But if any man wishes to remain in America, I shall see to it that he has a home, work of his liking, land that he may own by his own labors! If you will be free, stay in America!"

At his final words, a cheer went up from the American sailors hanging in the rigging, standing behind their captain, crowded about the railing. And after a short pause of bewilderment, the British seamen joined in the cry, giving a hoarse cheer for the captain, and three cheers for the new land of America.

Diana felt like cheering herself, but Sir Geoffrey's frosty look and her father's hand on her shoulder deterred her. Lord Somerville had come at the beginning of Captain McCullough's speech, and listened with a troubled, angry face to all he said.

Sailors' hats were tossed into the air, and Captain McCullough relaxed. "Dismissed! To your duties!" he said firmly, and they began to disperse.

Quietly, he ordered two seamen to escort Sir Geoffrey below.

"Badly timed," growled Lord Somerville. "I thought the storm would make them careless."

"Oh, Papa, did you know? Were you involved in this?" exclaimed Diana, disappointed in him. He frowned at her.

"And you, miss, return to your cabin. Why are you up here? You could have been hurt. Go below!"

She went down slowly, and sat thoughtfully in her cabin until Fred came to tell her breakfast was ready. She had much to think about.

Chapter 8

Long golden and blue days followed each other like sapphires hung lovingly on a golden chain. The short, purple-blue nights were hung with brilliant stars. Then June turned into July, and the days burned swiftly into each other. Soon, Diana thought, they would be in Boston, and what would she do then? It would depend on how her father and Sir Geoffrey were treated, she decided, and tried to dismiss worries from her mind. They had gotten themselves into political trouble; it was up to them to extricate themselves.

Of more concern to her were the dreams that kept weaving through her thoughts, day and night. She would waken, smiling, thinking of Jeremy McCullough and his rude embrace, his hard, warm kisses on her mouth. In the quiet of her cabin, it was not so bad, but when she leaned on the railing, remembering the hard pressure of his body against hers, the passion of that generous mouth against her lips—and then he came by with a smile and a word—then she would flush with embarrassment. She had no right to think so intimately about him. Once the voyage was over, she would probably never see him again. And she was engaged to Sir Geoffrey.

However, she could not seem to control her

mind. It was as wayward as the wind that swept her hair into tangles and whipped her cheeks into a rosy glow. As she paced the deck, talking with Eli Ulrich, she would suddenly recall how Jeremy McCullough had held her possessively against himself, had thrust his fingers through her hair, and had pressed his hand to her cheek and throat. And his eyes—they would go over her body in the thin muslin gowns that outlined her slim, rounded form. And she knew he approved of what he saw.

And she was glad, glad that she was lovely to his eyes, this brazen, laughing sea captain. When she chose a dress in the morning, and held it against herself, she would wonder whether or not he would like the color, the shape. Never had she dressed so anxiously for a man's approval. In the cool evenings, she often wore a blue velvet dress he liked, cut low, with a slim necklace of sapphires that had been her mother's. Sapphire earbobs swung from her delicate ears, her hair was drawn back in smooth golden wings, and the captain's green eyes seemed to blaze when he looked at her beside him.

She listened hungrily to Eli's stories of sailing with Captain McCullough. For hours at a time she paced the deck, and thought of him, and his free land. They were not for her, but she could not stop dreaming, wishing, hoping.

As they drew ever closer to the coast of North America, two lookouts hung from the tiny nest of the *Eagle*, watching as intently as if they expected an attack. Captain McCullough carried his long black spyglass with him constantly, and swept the ocean in all directions, his face grave.

"Why do you watch so, Captain?" Diana ventured to ask him one day, as he lowered the glass. "Surely you will see only Yankee ships here."

He leaned against the railing beside her, and studied her with a slight smile. "Not so, my lady," he said gravely. "You see, our ships are blocked from reaching our own ports. The British and the French both have imposed blockades, some in Europe, some here. We slip in and out, but at our risk. None can help us. The British paper blockade forbids any of us to come and go. Their actual ship blockade extends far out into the Atlantic, and if they can see us here, they will attack and capture if they can."

She gazed at him, wide-eyed and shocked. "But, sir, we are not at war!"

"No, God help us. But I fear the British Parliament will drive us to that extreme if they continue to forbid us to trade. We must trade or perish in New England. And the southern colonists suffer also, for lack of markets aboard for their cotton, hemp and tobacco."

"But Papa said there would be no war! He believes that peaceful trade can be continued—"

"I surely hope so. But doesn't your father also hope that we will give up trying to survive alone, and return to mother England?" His mouth twisted wryly at her look of dismay. "Yes, I think he has that idea. So do many others. They do not like their young sprig of a colony managing to survive on its own. But like many young sons of a possessive mother, young America would go out on her own and make her own fortunes. Mother must be convinced that son knows best for himself."

She smiled at his choice of words, and his green eyes warmed in response. He leaned companionably on the railing beside her, and pointed out a school of fish darting through the water. "Later on, when we come closer to land, you will see great clusters of sea gulls coming out to greet us. They can fly far from land, and they are our first sign that we approach a harbor."

"Sail—hoooo!" came the excited cry from a lookout. In an instant, Captain McCullough had his spyglass to his eye. "From the sou'east, Cap'n!"

He turned in that direction, to study the sail. Eli Ulrich ran up, and called for all hands on deck.

Another cry came. "She comes closer, Cap'n! She flies the flag of Italy!"

Diana began to relax, then saw the grim line of Jeremy's mouth. "Is—is that safe?" she asked anxiously.

He nodded at their own mast. The flag of Spain was being run up. "My lady, we all run up neutral-country flags until we are closer. I beg you, go below in safety, until we find out what country this is. Go quickly!"

She ran down to her cabin, trembling a little at the news that another sail might mean danger. In the peaceful weeks that had followed the battle between the *Ulysses* and the *Eagle*, Diana had almost managed to forget that day's grim sights.

She heard the pounding of the men as they ran about the deck, and the sound of the great guns being rolled out. They waited, she and Hester, wide-eyed and apprehensive, until they heard the cry, "She is American! She shows our flag, Cap'n!"

Diana's shoulders relaxed, and she leaned back on the bunk with a great sigh of relief. She heard Captain McCullough shout through the megaphone, "What ship are you?"

"The *Elsie*, out of New York!" came the cry from the other ship.

"Come aboard, and welcome! Have you news?"

"Much news, Captain McCullough!" came the reply.

Fred came to the door and tapped, grinning from ear to ear. "She's friendly, my lady, and her captain and mate will be boarding us with news. Captain McCullough, he says you and your father may come up and hear the news. There'll be entertaining today!"

Diana went up eagerly with the lad, to see the two ships maneuvering closer, the lines thrown out, the planks laid across. The first to come aboard the *Eagle* was a stout, red-faced sea captain with the keenest blue eyes she had ever seen. He held out his hand with a grin, and Captain McCullough took it.

"Captain Parker! Welcome aboard, it's been

two years since we've met!" There was warmth in
Jeremy's voice, and in the answering one.

"Oh, aye, much too long, Captain! But I hear
tales of you— I say, what is this? You carry a
lady?" His quick blue eyes had gone swiftly to
Diana, who stood near the stairs to her cabin.

Jeremy McCullough beckoned to the girl, and,
she came shyly forward. "My prisoner, and a fair
one," he grinned. "Lady Diana Somerville, may I
present Captain Parker of the brig *Elsie*. An old
friend and a good one."

Her hand was taken gently in his huge, rough
one, and pressed so slightly she thought he must
be afraid her bones would break. His blue eyes
passed shrewdly over her, and he nodded approval. Behind them Lord Somerville approached,
a scowl darkening the face below his formal wig.

He was introduced, and Captain Parker asked
politely as to their circumstances. He nodded as
Captain McCullough told of taking and sinking
the *Ulysses*.

The young first mate from the *Elsie* soon joined
them, accompanied by several sailors. Chairs were
brought up onto the deck of the *Eagle*, and they
sat about and conversed as though at a garden
party, thought Diana with amusement. She was
pleased at being placed at Captain McCullough's
right, and included in the conversation. The sailors were staring at her, and trying not to be
caught at it.

"May I ask a favor of you, Captain Parker?"
asked McCullough presently. "I am short of fresh

vegetables and fruits. Do you have some to spare?"

"Oh, aye, for I sail to St. Johns, a short voyage and with plenty of stores aboard. What will ye trade?"

"I have a great store of sherry and rum, along with wines of France. Will you have them?"

They struck a bargain instantly, much to Diana's surprise, and the two captains gave swift orders. The sailors immediately began carrying great boxes and barrels across the narrow planks, moving easily on their bare feet. The operation completed, the sailors sank down to the deck to listen frankly to their captains' conversations, or to wander off with sailors of the other ship, exchanging news and greetings, or smoking a friendly pipe.

"Now, Captain Parker, you said you had great news. We are becoming impatient to hear it."

"Oh, aye," said Captain Parker, puffing at his pipe, and looking uneasily at Lord Somerville, sitting on the other side of him. "Shall we go to your cabin, sir?"

"No, no, you may speak freely before my guests. If there is news that your sailors know, mine shall know it in minutes," said Jeremy with a laugh, and a wave of his hand at the full deck of gossiping men.

"Well, humphhh, yes, of course." He seemed to squirm on his chair for a minute. Diana felt a sudden intuition that the news would prove bad for herself and her father.

"Come, man, tell me. You have me agog," said Jeremy dryly.

"Well, no way to make it easier. We are at war with England."

Jeremy stared at him in silence for a long moment. Lord Somerville gave a great groan. "Oh, no, what goddamn foolishness, they would not do so!"

"It has been done, Lord Somerville, I regret to tell you," said Captain Parker formally. He turned to McCullough. "On June first President Madison asked Congress for a declaration of war. You know how much pressure he's suffered from the war hawks. He cited the impressment of American seamen, blockades of our ports, and so on. War was declared by Congress on June eighteen past."

"I feared it would come to this," Jeremy murmured thoughtfully.

"But it is nonsense!" cried Lord Somerville, in great agitation. "Our Parliament was coming to the point of ceasing to hinder trade. The manufacturing districts of Great Britain have begged for trade to be continued once again. They have been hurt gravely. I myself come on a trade mission—you have my papers, Captain, you know I speak the truth," and he gave McCullough a bitterly resentful look.

"They were not in time, evidently," said McCullough quietly. "They have talked and lingered when they should have acted. I know of the poverty and distress which the blockade has caused in England as well as America. If only it could have been peacefully settled! But the British have moved too slowly."

"You shall see we shall not move slowly in settling the war!" retorted Lord Somerville in rare fury. "You have a small Navy—Mr. Jefferson ordered it cut back to balance the budget. We shall sweep you from the seas, and you shall be punished for your impudence!"

"We shall see about that," McCullough said flatly, and turned once again to Parker. "Well, now, tell me the rest of the news. I have been away from home these four months."

To Diana's relief the subject was changed. The talk was of Congress, of other laws passed, of the harvest to come, of other captains Captain Parker had met. News was exchanged with great delight. Other sailors drifted by, exchanging their own news with a freedom Diana felt would not have been allowed on a British ship. Yet there was no lack of order. A second lieutenant was stationed at either end of the planks between the ships, and when anyone passed one way or another, salutes were exchanged and crisp directions given. When tobacco changed hands, it was paid for in coins, or traded for some other object of value.

Finally the talks were concluded. Wine and liquor were brought out, and entertainment was provided, to Diana's surprise and delight.

Sir Geoffrey was brought up, with two seamen stationed quietly behind him. He did not seem pleased by the favor, and stood surly and quiet during the demonstration that followed.

Seamen from both ships brought out their musical instruments. Some played mouth organs, most skillfully. Others had pipes, horns, drums, cymbals. A man from the *Elsie* brought a violin, which the men called a fiddle, and played it with great vigor and charm. The men formed patterns and danced for them, jigs and reels following each other rapidly, as though they vied with each other to perform the best.

The captains applauded the playing and dancing, calling out to their own men for encouragement. As two of the liveliest jigged across from each other, bobbing up and down like mad puppets, Jeremy called out, "Come on, Jimmy, lad, you have him licked!" And the other sailors of the *Eagle* laughed and egged on the red-faced sailors until they stopped and fell on the deck for sheer lack of breath.

Six men even formed a solemn set, and began to dance a formal movement. Jeremy joined in the clapping for rhythm, and Diana began to clap also, caught up in the merry dancing.

One of the sailors came over to her, bashful, but urged on by his mate. He bowed low. "My lady, will ye—I mean—will ye do us the honor of joining in on the dance?"

His eyes begged her also. She smiled and stood up. "I do not know this dance, but if you will but lead me I shall try it!"

"Diana!" growled her father. She did not turn her head.

Another man joined them, to make eight, and

they went round the set. They handled her very gently, as though she were made of porcelain, and the sailors clapped the rhythm while one called the moves. She was out of breath, but laughing, as they finally finished the set, and they applauded her, more for her joining them in such friendly fashion than for her skill in the intricate moves.

Dinner was brought up on trays for the captains and their guests. They ate heartily, drank toasts to the ships, to America, and gallantly to England. Somerville relaxed enough to answer this one gracefully.

Diana ate and drank quietly, listening to the merry conversation. She sensed the great friendship between the captains, the complete trust between the sailors of the two American ships. Only Sir Geoffrey was sullen, and after dinner he went below. Diana was not sure if he left of his own will, or whether the captain had tired of his scowling face.

After dinner, the music began again. Once more the pipes were played sweetly to the bounding of nimble feet. Fred excelled in one dance, and subsided at Diana's feet with a laugh when it was finished, his face flushed and proud.

Jeremy beckoned to the man who played the fiddle, who bent to hear his wish. "Do you know a waltz, my lad?" he asked.

"Oh, aye, sir, I know a fine one," and he began to play. Jeremy stood, and bowed to Diana, a mocking gleam in his eye.

"My lady? Will you honor me?"

Her father, mellowed by wine and conversation, did not object this time. She smiled, gave Jeremy her hand, and rose gracefully, her white dress floating about her. The sailors stood aside to watch, silently, as they moved about the deck, whirling around and around in the graceful movements. The music went on and on, sweetly romantic on the sea air, and the pipes joined in tentatively, with a wistful note.

As they ended, the applause jolted her back to reality. She had been lost in a dream as they danced, held closely to Jeremy's hard form. They had met in a ballroom, danced the waltz, and now she was his prisoner—in more ways than one, she thought ruefully, as they moved about the deck. He released her, escorted her back to her chair. He lifted her hand to his lips, and for a moment she felt his mouth pressed to her fingers.

Then he released her, and bowed again.

"Very pretty, very pretty," cried Captain Parker. "I must learn it. My wife will be amazed at me!"

"It pays to amaze the ladies at times," said Jeremy, with a laugh. They talked again, easily, over the music. But the sailors were glancing at the sky now, as it turned to red, scarlet, purple.

"Ah, it is dusk, we must be on our way," said Captain Parker with regret. "Jeremy, lad, it's been a fine visit. I thank you for the wines and such—and the pleasure of your company, my lady!" He gave Diana a deep bow, and she rose and curtsied in response.

They shook hands all round, then climbed the planks back to their ship. The lines were cast off, the sails loosened from their binding. The ships moved apart slowly, as the sunset crimsoned the western sky.

Diana leaned on the railing and wistfully watched the *Elsie* draw away from them. The sky deepened to purple, and the first stars twinkled against its velvet setting. The white sails moved farther away, and farther still, until she could no longer make out the shape of them.

It had been one of the happiest days of her life, she decided, as she watched the ship disappearing. The disarming friendliness of the sailors, the music and dancing, the warmth of the conversation, her dance with Jeremy. . . . She saw him now, crisply issuing orders to the officer of the deck, conferring with a sailor, glancing up into the masts critically. Then he strode over to her.

"We will have a light supper, Lady Diana, if you are ready?"

She smiled, took his arm, and went below with him to the dining cabin. Lord Somerville soon joined them, mellowed by the gay afternoon, but still grave.

"This is a sad business, this war declaration," he began at once. Diana sighed and leaned back. Back to business, she thought, and the afternoon's warmth would soon be gone. But Jeremy gave her a little wink of encouragement even as he answered her father. And she remembered the hard pressure of his arm as he had waltzed with her. She had that to recall, that memory to cherish, as the brig *Eagle* sailed on toward the American shore.

Chapter 9

Captain Talbot had been ill for several days. He had missed the visit of the *Elsie* and lay below in a cabin with a heavy cold and cough, brought on when he had remained on deck during the rainstorm. Diana included the captain in the sick visits she made with Eli Ulrich, and he seemed very grateful to her. She fed him sops dipped in broth, and hot mulled wine, which seemed to ease his discomfort. But the fever had lingered for a time.

Several of the wounded were now up and about, and able to help with the more gravely wounded. Eli worried over the man who had lost an arm, and conferred gravely with Captain McCullough over his misfortune.

"We shall be in Boston harbor in a matter of days, God willing," Jeremy replied. "Then he shall have the best doctors we can find. Until then, help him as you can." Eli nodded gravely, and Jeremy escorted Diana back up on deck.

"How do you manage?" she asked impulsively. "Surely it is not unusual for you to have men injured in battles. Do you lose many?"

He tucked Diana's hand into the crook of his arm, and they strolled about the deck in the hazy sunlight of early noon.

"The men will fight hard, my lady. They would

rather fight and be injured—even killed—than be captured and impressed. Too many of our lads have been carried away for years, and sometimes lost forever. The ones who manage to return tell horrible tales of cruelty, beatings, torture even," he said, with a light pressure on her arm as she shuddered. "I am sorry to tell you this, Lady Diana, but you should know the truth."

"I am sorry, too," she whispered. "How can people be so inhuman to each other? There is enough sorrow in the world, with disease, and storms— Must men fight each other also?"

He bent to her, and murmured in her ear, "You have tears in your lovely eyes, my lady. I would fight much to earn such for myself!"

"Oh, you are but teasing me again!" She turned away impatiently, tugging at her arm to free herself.

He held her the more firmly. "No, no, I do not," he said quietly. "But you asked about our wounded. The next ship I take out will be larger, of thirty guns or more. She is being built in our shipyards now. With her, I shall sign on more men, and a surgeon among them. Since we must go to war, we shall be prepared."

She was shocked into silence. He would go out again, and again! And her country was at war with his! Back home in England, she might one day casually open a gazette, to find his name in the columns, to hear of his injury, his capture—even his death! She could not speak at the thought.

She thought of him in one of those large frigates, guns blasting in red fury at another ship, the masts shredded, the sails torn from the rigging. And Jeremy—injured—bloody—like those men she had seen the day of the battle. Or lying in fever below decks—

Eli Ulrich came up to him with a question. He bowed and left her. She leaned against the rail, and closed her eyes. She felt rather ill, but not from the motion of the ship.

Was it her imagination, or did the sky darken? She opened her eyes to see ahead of them some light mist above the water, and the sun disappearing behind the clouds.

She bit her lips to keep back tears. She had never in her life, not since her mother's death, felt so wretched, so alone and forlorn. With her was a great anxiety she feared would never leave her. This gay and gallant Yankee might one day be captured, tortured, wounded—killed. And something inside herself would die on that day, she thought. She pressed her hand to her cheek, wondering, amazed, dismayed. She loved him, oh, she loved him. But it was all so impossible.

She leaned there for some time, tormented by her thoughts. Yet she felt exalted also. She had thought she was too cold to feel love. She had thought to marry Sir Geoffrey, endure his embraces, bear his child, turn with relief to the arranging of flowers, the direction of his household. Never to love, never to feel anything but cool interest in anyone.

And now she loved! She heard Jeremy's voice

raised in command, and she thrilled to the sound of his deep, sure tones. She turned to gaze at him, and found him standing near the wheel, gazing out to sea, the spyglass raised to his eye. She would always think of him like this, she believed, imprinting the scene on her mind. She gazed at him, at the bronze-gold of his hair ruffled in the wind, the tan of his face as he lifted his head to call to the lookout. The steadiness of his body, braced against the tilt of the wooden deck. The cut of his dark blue coat, the length of his legs in the white knee breeches. The gold epaulets on his shoulders. Oh, he was a fine figure of a man, she thought with a sigh of pleasure, and of regret.

He was not for her. But she did love him, and her heart yearned to tell of that love. But it must not be told. She was engaged to another man. And besides, the Yankee captain showed no signs of yearnings for her. He would race about the seas for years, and perhaps one day choose a girl to his liking, one of the free young American girls, probably.

Luncheon was announced, and she went below. The captain did not join them. There was some difficulty about a sail. She answered her father absently when he spoke to her, and for once was glad of the presence of Sir Geoffrey, released from his cabin.

Sir Geoffrey, infuriated at being held prisoner aboard ship, was now chafing at the thought of being brought into Boston as a prisoner. Diana listened to their discussion of various ways of handling the problem when they arrived, and thought that for once they would have to bow to whatever the Americans decided.

In the night, a storm came up, and Diana found the deck rain-washed the next morning. The ship had rocked all night, and she had wondered if they were in for another heavy storm.

Diana walked slowly about the deck, wary of the wet wooden planks. Fred came up to her cheerily, and gave her his shy grin.

"There be fog ahead, miss, we can see it in the distance." He pointed toward large banks of fog gathering in the north and west.

"What does that mean, Fred? Will we be delayed?"

"Don't know, my lady, it depends on the wind and how much we can see. We sail by compass, so we shan't lose our way," and he proudly went on to explain about compasses and fixing positions.

Rain had begun to spatter the deck. Diana took shelter under an overhang and, with her cloak drawn close about her, watched as the men ran about to take in sails and tie down barrels.

Jeremy found her there, and peered under the overhang to smile at her. "Well, well, it's a bright-eyed kitten in the storm," he drawled, laughing softly. "Won't you run inside, my lady?"

"Oh, must I?" she asked, her heart racing as he came closer to her.

"Not unless it really pours. We don't want you catching cold as Captain Talbot did. So you enjoy our ship, do you?" And he touched her rain-washed cheek. "You are as fresh as a rose, with dewdrops on your petals!"

"Oh, Captain, how you flatter!" She laughed, hoping he would not see how he flustered her.

He gave her a boyish grin. "You bring out the words, my lady. You would inspire even a poor sea captain to poetry. Ah, I'm glad you enjoy the sea. You'd make a fine wife for a sailor!"

Her heart raced more rapidly, but she knew he was only teasing her. She spoke the more tartly: "What, so the sailor might leave her at home, while he goes adventuring? Not for me, thank you!"

"You are right, of course, though some sailors take their wives to sea. I know captains who take their wives with them all the way to China and back. The wives assist in the bookkeeping, and in purchasing precious cargoes in China. But you are too delicate a lady for that, I think. You should be kept at home and cosseted."

She felt strangely hurt by his words. She tossed her head, and the cloak fell back from her golden hair. "Too delicate, am I? Have I not endured this voyage well? And it was my first!"

He drew the cloak back over her head with a caressing hand. "Yes, you have done well. And it shall not be your last voyage, I think."

"Of course not. I must sail back to England one day soon."

"If we let you go," he said, with a mischievous twinkle. "Perhaps you shall remain my prisoner for—"

"Sail—hoooooo!" came the lookout's cry. The mischief was gone from Jeremy's face, swept away by the alert look of a hawk. "Go below, and swiftly!" he said to her.

She ran down to her cabin, and Hester looked up anxiously from her sewing. "Oh, what is it, my lady?" she cried.

"They had spied a sail. Probably friendly," said Diana, removing her cloak, and brushing back her blonde hair in front of the small mirror. Her eyes were strangely bright.

She left the cabin door open and listened. She heard the sharp cries of the lookout, the swift orders from the captain and first mate.

"She's a big one—and British, Cap'n!" finally came the shout.

Diana ran to the window and peered out. She gasped to see how close the ship was. It had three sets of sails, and even as she watched the guns were run out. From across the waters came the commanding order, "Strike your colors!"

"Oh, it is British!" she whispered, seeing the Union Jack at the mast. Once that would have brought a thrill of pride, but now, remembering her conversation with Jeremy— Oh, they *could* not be captured! She could not bear the thought of Jeremy becoming a prisoner, or any other of her friends aboard the Yankee brig.

"Lay on the sail!" came Jeremy's clear command.

"Do you strike?" came impatiently from across the waters.

The ship seemed to bound through the waters. The sky was black with storm, and ahead of them lay the fog and mist. Diana caught her breath, watching the British frigate draw closer.

She clutched at the nearest object, the dresser, as the smaller ship bounded up and down the waves, into the troughs, then on the crests. She forced herself to get out the valises, and stuff into them her mirrors, brushes, jewels, and powder. There was going to be a storm, and probably a battle. It would be best to fasten everything down. She thrust the valises into the wardrobe, and shut the door. Hester was moaning on her bed, her eyes tight shut with fear.

Fred came down to the door, his feet bare.

"Please, my lady, Cap'n says—" He paused for breath. "Will you please not to move about, nor talk? All of us is not to wear boots nor shoes, not strike against metal, if you will."

"Oh, why is that?" She whispered, because he had done so.

"We're going to try for the fog, to get away—"

"Get away? How?"

"I don't know, my lady. The cap'n just said to tell you to stay safe, and not to move about the ship, lessn you have your shoes off." And then he was gone.

Puzzled, she removed her small boots, and tied on soft slippers. Then she hurried to the windows, and gasped to see the British ship drawing closer to them, her guns raised.

Then into the silence of the fog and darkness

came the boom of the guns, cracking fire and smoke across the small distance of the sea between them.

They were fired upon! The British ship raked them, drawing alongside and past them, and then was beyond them in the fog. Diana heard the crack of a mast as it toppled, the shouts of the men, silenced by a crisp order. "Quiet! Be silent!"

A man stumbled down the stairs, leaving a trail of blood. His face was ghastly as he clutched at his injured arm. Diana gasped, then rushed to him, and put a supporting arm about the man.

"Miss," he whispered. "You shouldn't be about—"

"I'll help you below," she whispered back. He nodded, unable to argue with her. His young face was streaked with black grime, and the eyes that looked out from that blackened face were full of horror.

She took him down to the large cabin where the wounded lay. Only the most gravely injured were still there. The others must have gone on deck, or to the guns below deck to help.

She helped him to a chair, then went to get bandages, water, and ointment. Eli Ulrich could not be spared; she must help.

She removed his shirt. He was rocking back and forth, forcing himself not to moan. The captain had said not to speak, and the young man was trying his best not to make a sound, but sweat sprang out on his forehead in his agony.

She washed the wound and whispered, "It is

not broken, lad." At her words, he gave her a ghastly smile. She picked out the bits of shot from his arm, wincing for him as she penetrated his flesh. Then she washed the wound again before applying ointment and bandages.

Another man staggered down the stairs, and fell to the floor just as she was finishing. She braced herself and knelt beside him. The young man opened his eyes, to stare at her, dazed.

"The cap'n, he's been hit," he whispered.

Her heart must have stopped completely, she was sure. There was no beat, no pulse. Then it began again, racing with such a fury that she felt faint.

"The captain—where did he get it?" whispered the other sailor. The wounded stirred in their bunks where they had lain silent.

"In the shoulder. First off. But he's going on. Gonna try to get away in the fog," the sailor explained wearily. Diana bent to examine his leg, which appeared to have sustained the worst injury.

Blood was pounding in her head, she felt dizzy and weak, but she must help, she must help. It was all she could do now. But Jeremy was hit— Jeremy was wounded—

She cleansed the wound and examined it carefully by the light of the smoky lamp. It was finally bandaged and the sailor helped to a bunk. Then Diana went up to her cabin again. She scrubbed her hands carefully, then hurried to the porthole to peer out to the deck.

The ship was silent.

There was no clink of metal on metal, no cheerful shouts of sailors. No booted feet strode on the deck above her head. Even the creak of the sails seemed stilled.

Was everyone dead? Did she sail on a ghost ship? All sorts of nervous questions raced through her mind, making her shudder. At the window, she watched as the ship sailed into still denser fog. Soon she could see nothing. The other ship seemed to have disappeared. Where was it? Hiding in the fog, waiting to pounce and fire on them again? And where was Jeremy?

The thought of him wounded and suffering finally drove her to disobey orders. She gathered up the ointment, a jar of water, and some bandages, and went silently to the stairs. Above her was fog, dense and white. She climbed the stairs, and was amazed to find that on deck she could not even see the wheel from the distance of the stairway.

She groped forward through the ever-thickening fog. She saw the mast that had been broken, and now lay across the deck in a tangle of sails. She skirted that, and finally found her way to the wheel. And there was Jeremy, a crude sling holding his arm to his chest, blood on his forehead, his mouth tight and hard.

He saw her and opened his eyes in amazement. But he did not speak. She came up, sat down on the deck, carefully set down the jars so they made no sound, and beckoned to him. A grin slashed his powder-blackened face, and he sat down beside her.

Sailors stood all around, but no one moved or spoke. All were watching, waiting, as the *Eagle* slid silently through the heaving waters.

Diana took the sling from Jeremy's neck, and unfastened his jacket. The sight of the wound on his upper arm made her tremble. But she gritted her teeth and opened his shirt all the way. With a piece of cloth, she carefully washed around the wound. When the surrounding flesh was clean, she looked closer. There was metal embedded in the arm.

She found her small instrument and used it delicately to remove the metal, dropping it into her pocket so nothing would clink to the deck with a betraying sound. Jeremy was watching her gravely, his green eyes almost gray in the dimness. His hair was mussed, his forehead covered with sweat. He had never looked so arrogant or so handsome, she thought, as when he sat wounded on his own quarterdeck.

When she was sure all the metal had been removed from his arm, she washed the wound with a cloth. Then she smoothed on the ointment delicately with her fingers, making sure it went deep into the wound. She almost gasped, thinking of his pain.

Finally the wound was bandaged, his shirt and jacket eased over it. The sling was readjusted. He nodded his thanks, smiling into her anxious eyes. Then he leaned forward and very gently pressed his mouth to her lips. When he drew back, she gathered up her bottles and cloth with trembling hands.

She was still sitting there when he stood and turned to Eli Ulrich, who had approached on bare feet. "Still hear them sails behind us," whispered Eli.

Jeremy nodded. "Behind us to the east, then?"

Eli nodded. Jeremy pointed to the northwest then, and the pilot swung the wheel gently in that direction. They stood and waited. Diana sat among them, as though frozen.

An hour went by. A sailor came to her on Eli's direction and shyly showed her the wound on his head. She bathed and dressed it, glad to have something to do. He thanked her with a smile, and she nodded to him gratefully.

Eli came again. "I think we've lost her," he whispered to Jeremy.

The captain nodded again. "Take my lady below. We'll stay on course now. No sounds, mind."

Eli escorted Diana below, and she went, conscious that Jeremy was watching her as long as the fog permitted. She reached her cabin and whispered, "I must go down and see how the two injured sailors are doing."

Eli went with her, and they found the two men dozing but feverish. They tended to them, and to the other gravely injured one, and then she returned to her cabin, to endure an uneasy afternoon and evening. The fog pressed thick about the windows, but that made them safe—didn't it?

Fred brought their supper to the cabin on a wooden tray. It was only thick wooden bowls of soup, with lavish slices of bread and butter. "We can't serve dinner tonight, my lady, Cap'n's apologies," he murmured.

"No need to apologize. This is grand." He cheered up a bit under her radiant smile.

"I think we lost them in the fog, but the cap'n says we mun be careful for a time. Other ships about, might be British."

She gulped a little, then summoned a cheerful reply. "We shall all have to be careful then, not be captured by the terrible British!" She made a face, and he stifled a giggle behind his hand, like a child.

After they had eaten, and Fred had removed the tray, there was nothing to do but go to bed. The night passed slowly, and the next day found the ship still shrouded in fog.

Diana realized she had not given her father a thought, and wondered if he and Sir Geoffrey had been confined. Sir Arnold had also disappeared.

Fred said simply, "Oh, they be locked in their cabins, my lady. They would walk about in boots, and not observe the cap'n's rules, so they be locked in until we reach harbor."

"When will that be?"

He only shrugged to indicate he did not know. But she was permitted the range of the ship, and went up once, shyly, to see how Jeremy did. He greeted her with his quick radiant smile.

She examined his wound, and was relieved to

find it had not grown hot with fever. These sea-men were amazing, she thought; perhaps it was the salty air which helped them.

The men continued to whisper, or talked not at all. The lookouts clung to their eagle's nest high above the deck, scanning the sea but seeing little through the thick mist. The ship would make more rapid progress today, though, for the waters seemed calmer.

How clever Jeremy had been, slipping away from that huge British frigate in the fog! He had seen the mist coming, and managed to make use of it. What a seaman he was, she thought, with pride.

Another day and night had passed before Diana awakened to the sight of sunlight outside her port-hole. But as the morning dawned clear, she felt no relief. Without the fog, how could they elude the British?

Now she realized something else had changed during the night: the ship no longer trembled be-neath her feet. When she stood up, she almost fell over, so accustomed was she to swaying with the deck beneath her feet. It was not swaying!

She ran over to the porthole and stared out to see—a city outside! They were docked in some port, and other masts met her view. Just beyond their ship was an extensive shipyard, and beyond that houses, and more houses, and tall buildings.

She washed and dressed hastily. Hester was all excitement, wondering where they could be. "And may I never have to set foot on another ship, my lady!" she said fervently. "Nasty, smelly, sickly things they be!"

Diana wanted to remind Hester that they still had the journey home to England to make. But the thought gave her no pleasure either. So she only smiled, and shook her head.

They settled back to wait and see what would happen, and all too soon, it seemed, the pounding of boots on the deck, the whine of winches, reminded them they were back in civilization.

Diana thought she would miss the sunny days on deck, the sway of the ship under her feet, the musical cries of the sailors, the purple-blue nights, and the clear brilliant stars. And Jeremy.

A light tattoo on the door made her sit up straight. It was pushed open and Jeremy stood there, fine in a uniform of blue and buff, his white knee breeches immaculate. His cocked hat was tucked under his arm, which still rested in a sling. His grin was wide and happy.

"My lady! Welcome to Boston!"

Chapter 10

Diana could hear cheering as she packed. Fred kept her informed on developments. The crowd onshore was cheering the ship, and the cheering swelled as the Yankee captain appeared, and went down the gangplank to shore.

"There be men coming on board to inspect," Fred said breathlessly on his third trip to her cabin. "They will be talking to you, my lady, and to Lord Somerville and Sir Geoffrey."

"Oh—because we are prisoners," she said blankly. She had almost forgotten that.

Fred nodded unhappily. "But I'm sure Captain McCullough won't let them be nasty, or anything," he said, with comforting confidence in his captain.

Diana wondered how it would have been had the tables been turned, and Captain McCullough and his men arrived in England as their prisoners. No nice treatment for them, she decided, and she should not expect much either.

Presently her father came to escort her to the deck. He looked grim and tired, his coat wrinkled, his wig clapped on his head with none of his accustomed care.

She picked up her valise, but Fred would not let her carry it. He was eager to be of help. When her father went on ahead, Diana slipped a gold guinea into Fred's hand, and whispered, "How can I thank you for your goodness to us?"

"Oh, my lady, it was my pleasure, I'm sure," he said, and wanted to refuse the coin until she insisted he keep it.

On deck, several grave-looking men stood about, two in dark, snuff-brown coats and one in uniform. They were talking to Captain McCullough. He seemed to be protesting, shaking his head, but one of the other men appeared to be persuasive.

Jeremy turned to Diana. "They wish you to go with them, my lady," he said formally. "I am sending your gear to a friend's home. Nathaniel Bellows and his family will be happy to house you and your father, and your servants. I shall call upon you there, and make sure you are comfortable."

"Oh, are we not to be in prison, then?"

His eyes blazed with anger. "Of course not!" he said sharply. "I will not permit it! Do but answer their questions frankly. This matter is none of your doing. And your father is on a peaceful diplomatic mission. They understand that."

He seemed very brisk and official today, not the warm, teasing man she had known. And suddenly Diana felt she would never be sure of anything again. She shook the hand of Eli Ulrich, who beamed at her and murmured that she should keep her chin up. Fred seemed on the verge of tears as she left the *Eagle*. She shook hands with several of the others, smiled and waved at them.

Her father seemed very cross. He hastened down the plank as though glad to quit the ship. Sir Geoffrey was silent, his face dark with resentment.

They were escorted into carriages, Diana with her maid, her father and Sir Geoffrey in another, and their luggage went off in another direction. Captain Talbot had already been taken away. She leaned forward for one last look at the brig *Eagle*, and saw Captain McCullough standing on the deck, his head bright in the sunlight. She was glad that she had one last glimpse of him.

The Britishers were taken to a large building, smart with white paint. Inside, they were shown to an office where a magistrate in a sober dark suit and bright neckcloth received them. By her father's disdainful look, Diana realized he did not think the man a gentleman.

They were questioned separately. Diana waited nervously with Hester in an outer room. Tea was brought to her by a young man in a blue smock. She thanked him and drank eagerly. She was not sure when she would enjoy a cup of tea again. Were not the Americans against tea now? She had read that they had tossed tea overboard at the beginning of the Revolution.

After about two hours, her father emerged from the office, his face crimson, his eyes blazing angrily. Diana felt her heart sink to her fashionable boots.

"Damned impertinent," he muttered, and sank into a chair. "Doubted everything I said!"

"Oh, dear," murmured Diana. Now it was her turn to go in. She lifted her chin, swallowed hard, and followed the clerk into the magistrate's office.

One man sat behind the deck, an elderly man with a kind, weary face. A younger man stood near the door, and sprang up to hold a chair for her. She thanked him and seated herself with a rustle of her blue silk skirts.

"Lady Diana Somerville?" the older man said, giving her a keen look.

"Yes, sir."

"I understand you accompany your father and your—ah—fiancé to America?"

"That is correct, sir."

"We have discussed the matter of the *Ulysses* firing upon the brig *Eagle* with Captain Talbot. Were you about when the decision was made to fire upon the American ship?"

"Yes, sir." She clasped her hands tightly.

"Do you know whose decision it was to fire? Was it that of Captain Sir Arnold Talbot?"

She hesitated. She hated to say anything against Sir Geoffrey, yet it was not entirely the captain's fault.

The younger man interrupted. "She is probably not versed in military matters, sir!"

"No, sir, I am not," said Diana faintly, as they both looked at her.

"Ah—your father is on a trade mission to America?"

She was relieved at the change of topic, as her interrogator moved some papers about on his desk.

"Yes, sir. He wished to improve trade. I believe he mentioned cotton, tobacco, and hemp in particular."

"Ah—yes. Do you know aught of the matter of the manufacturing districts in England, who pleaded for more trade?"

"Oh—I have read the gazettes, sir. I know it is being argued in Parliament that they begged for more trade, rather than a blockade, which aided no one."

"And did you know that America was at war with England when you began your journey, my lady?"

"No, sir, not until we were informed by the captain of an American vessel whom we met upon the way."

The younger man went over and muttered earnestly to the older one. Diana shifted uneasily. She had never been questioned so before. They were polite, but she thought they seemed wary of her.

"Well, well, we may wish to question you again, my lady," said the older one. "For now, Mr. Bellows has asked the privilege of entertaining you in his home. You understand that you are not to leave Boston except on our express authority, and you may not sail for England until permission is given."

"Am I—a prisoner, sir?"

"Well, only in a manner of speaking, my lady," he said, smiling. "So fair a lady should not be a prisoner of any but the god of love!"

He stood up as he spoke. She blushed crimson, and finally stood also. "You may go, my lady, and thank you," he went on. "May you enjoy your stay in our fair city, though you may not think it compares with London."

"Oh, thank you, sir, it seemed very handsome indeed, from the carriage," she managed to say politely, as she was handed from the room.

"That was short," growled her father as she came out. "I suppose we are all off to prison now! I shall complain—"

"No, indeed, Lord Somerville!" said the younger man. "It is my pleasure to escort you to the home where you will remain during your stay in Boston. Another gentleman has offered to house Sir Geoffrey Loring and Captain Talbot. We hope you will all be most comfortable."

Sir Geoffrey glared at him. Diana's father snorted. Ashamed of the men's lack of manners, Diana turned to the man.

"You are most kind, sir. I am afraid you would not be nearly so well treated should you be a prisoner in London. May I express our gratitude to you, and to Captain McCullough for his most courteous treatment of us on his brig."

Captain Talbot did not try to hide his grin at her father's chagrin and her fiancé's stare. The young American bowed deeply, and offered her his arm to the carriage.

Lady Diana regretted her impulsiveness as the carriage pulled up to admit them. She had best mind her tongue, no matter how strongly she felt. She was soon to be under her father's charge again, and he did not appreciate disobedience.

The carriages rattled over the cobblestoned streets of Boston, past the docks, where she cast a long, wistful look at the *Eagle* and the tall, graceful ships that surrounded her. Then they were climbing a hill into a residential district, where they passed houses of increasing size and grandeur. Some were gray, some a bright blue, some white with green shutters.

The carriages finally pulled up in front of a fine yellow house with green shutters and large multi-paned windows. The roof was framed with a widow's walk and topped with chimneys. It was a two-story house, with single-story wings to either side, rather kindly in appearance, like a stout woman with arms outheld to her charges.

They alighted and went up to the door. The carved doors were flung open even as they approached, and out came a lady who matched the house. She was middle-aged, with dark hair and eyes, plump and merry, with cheeks like ripe apples.

"There you are, there you are, I expected you two hours ago!" she said. "May I introduce myself? Mrs. Maria Bellows of this household, and right glad to have you here!"

Lord Somerville drew himself up and looked down his long nose at her. "Lord Somerville, at

your service, madam!" he said frostily, and made
her a brief bow.

Diana smiled at the woman. "You are very courteous to give us house room, madam," she said
quietly. "I am afraid it will be a nuisance for you."

"No indeed, no indeed, Mr. Bellows and I are
proud to have you. And Jeremy McCullough said
it must be, so it must. Come in and see your
rooms." And she beckoned them in with a friendly
manner, in spite of Lord Somerville's coldness.

Maria Bellows directed a neat maid in a black
uniform to escort Lord Somerville and his valet to
their rooms in the east wing. She herself accompanied Diana and Hester to rooms on the second
floor.

"I thought you would be more comfortable
here, Lady Diana," she said, flinging open the
door to a suite of rooms. She entered and looked
sharply about as though to find a fleck of dust, or
a chair out of place, then smiled on finding all in
order. "Yes, yes, it is ready," she said with satisfaction.

The rooms were small, but looked immensely
comfortable to Diana after the cramped quarters
on the brig. The sitting room was decorated in
blue trimmed with rose, with a small blue satin
sofa and matching chairs, a rose carpet with a flo-
ral print. The draperies were of a simple chintz
fabric, blue with white flowers. Two of the windows had been flung open to admit the air, and
Diana could smell the gardens outside, the roses

and honeysuckle, some herbs, and a starry white flower she did not recognize.

She commented on it, and Mrs. Bellows giggled. "Oh, that is tobacco; we grow it in the gardens. Isn't it odd, and it smells ever so nice."

She opened the door to Diana's bedroom, and Diana noted with a sigh of satisfaction a good-sized, plump bed, with four posters supporting a blue silk canopy. White netting hung over the silk.

"That's for the summer nights," explained Mrs. Bellows. "We do get night moths and mosquitoes, and you'd best pull the net down about the bed at nights. I do hope there is enough room for your dresses and such." And she looked anxiously at the one sturdy, rosewood wardrobe that the room contained.

"It all looks comfortable and beautiful. I apologize for intruding on your household again, Mrs. Bellows. It is so very kind of you and Mr. Bellows to entertain us."

Mrs. Bellows grew quite rosy with pleasure. "Indeed, Lady Diana, it is a joy to me! I love company, and my three girls can scarce wait to make your acquaintance. I told them not to make nuisances of themselves, and you are to tell me at once if they do!" she added darkly.

Maria Bellows bustled off to see that Hester found her bedroom, and that the servants were bringing up the trunks, valises, and hatboxes. Diana sank into an overstuffed chair and closed her eyes with relief. She still swayed from the motion of the ship, and the interview with the magistrates had been rather unnerving.

Were they really prisoners? The Americans had been courteous, but had made clear that she and her father were not to leave Boston. She wondered if guards had been set in front of the house, but could not stir herself to go and find out for herself. She would discover that in time.

Hester returned presently. "Mrs. Bellows seems a very pleasant and kind lady, for an American," she said in surprise.

Diana smiled. "I think many of the Americans are very kind—and thoughtful," she said dreamily. Hester eyed her keenly, and Diana roused herself. She must get up, help unpack, wash and dress again in something lighter. The day was quite warm.

Hester busied herself unpacking some of the gowns, and hanging them in the vast wardrobe. Diana washed and changed to a white muslin dress with blue ribbons at her waist, and a double row of frills about the hem and wrist.

"Mrs. Bellows said as how luncheon would be served at one o'clock, my lady," Hester said presently. "She will send up a tray if you should wish. Or you might come to the dining room on the ground floor."

"I'll go down," said Diana. "I'm anxious to meet her little girls."

She went down presently, her gown trailing on the steps of the rosewood staircase, and found herself the object of attention of three great pairs of brown eyes. The Bellows girls had come from a drawing room off the main hallway, and were gazing at her frankly. They were not little at all, she found to her amusement. One was about her age, the other two slightly younger.

The eldest came forward while her sisters giggled nervously.

"Lady Diana? May I introduce myself? I am Jennie Bellows, and we are so glad you have come!" She held out her hand, and Diana took it, studying the girl's lively face. Jennie had Mrs. Bellows' dark hair and eyes, her round, merry face, and motherly air. She drew the other two forward. "My sister Amy, and my youngest sister Dora."

"How do you do? I am so happy to meet you, and thank you for your hospitality," said Diana, shaking hands with them all. They had a vigorous way of shaking hands, new to her.

"Did you really get captured by Captain McCullough?" burst out the youngest, Dora, her eyes fascinated.

"Dora, do not ask personal questions!" scolded Jennie. "You know Mummy does not like it."

"Oh, I do not mind on this occasion," smiled Diana. "Yes, we were all captured from the *Ulysses*. However, I found the captain and his crew most kind and courteous. The captain gave his cabin to me and my maid. His first mate, Mr. Ulrich, was most generous in his time, and told me much of the sea and the way of ships."

"He's so terribly attractive!" Amy said breathlessly.

"Mr. Ulrich?" asked Diana, a twinkle in her blue eyes. She gave Jennie a swift look.

"No, no, Captain McCullough! We would have *fainted* if we had been *captured* by him. Oh, he's so very dangerously gallant!" sighed Dora.

"Girls, girls, are you keeping Lady Diana in the hallway?" Their mother's voice made them guilty at once, and she swept into the hall with a reproving shake of her head. "Pray, enter, Lady Diana, and forgive the girls. They are all gossips, all. I do not know what to do with them, in truth."

Diana was led into the sunny dining room, where she met her host. Nathaniel Bellows was a stocky, hearty man, of some forty-five years. His own dark hair shone unpowdered. His brown eyes twinkled with pride over his lively daughters and wife. She soon learned he was a merchant in silks and woolens, and a wealthy one from the looks of the house.

Her father did not appear. He had retired with a tray to his rooms. Diana was not sorry; the company was so gracious to her that she did not want their merriment spoiled by her father's icy manner.

"I should have swooned at being his prisoner!" Amy resumed immediately after the introductions. "He is so handsome, half of the girls in Boston are in love with him!"

Several pairs of brown eyes fastened on Diana, watching her every flicker of emotion. "Indeed? He is certainly an excellent sea captain," she said. "Thank you, I should like some beans. I tasted them first on the brig, and found them delicious. I hope to learn how to make several of the American dishes while I am here."

She managed to change the subject from the dangerous captain to food. Mrs. Bellows was pleased when Diana praised the roast lamb and mint jelly, the green salad from their garden, the pudding she called "Indian," made of corn and molasses.

After luncheon, Nathaniel Bellows returned to his office, which was some distance from the house. He walked back and forth twice a day, he said, and Diana detected a note of pride in his voice.

The women removed to the drawing room after the meal. Diana was pleased to find it was a beautiful but comfortable room, with a red carpet, shining rosewood and satinwood furniture, and a small piano in one corner. Jennie played, with a nice feeling, and Amy sang, with some giggling. Dora sat near Diana, and fixed her with devouring eyes, her every gesture, her every comment taken in and swallowed whole.

They had an easy informal way about them that made her feel as comfortable as Eli Ulrich and Fred had. Mrs. Bellows asked her if she preferred coffee or tea, and rambled on about her husband's work, the church nearby, the possibility of a party some afternoon soon to introduce Diana to some friends.

She might have been an honored guest in their home, rather than a prisoner inflicted on their hospitality. She relaxed, and chatted with them as easily as she would have with any of her own friends. How very pleasant they were, she thought, as she went upstairs later to rest for a time. She tried to suppress her curiosity about where Jeremy was now, and what he was doing, and whether he had seen a doctor about his wounds. She might never see him again—but she had to stop thinking about that.

Chapter 11

The days slid past quite pleasantly for Diana. Her father remained irritable and worried. He and Sir Geoffrey were trying to find out their position, whether it was worth remaining in America to salvage any part of their mission, or whether to bend their efforts to returning to England.

For Diana, the situation was different. Maria Bellows invited some of her female friends for tea one afternoon, and proudly asked Diana to be introduced into their society. It was a happy time for her.

About a dozen ladies of all ages came. One tiny woman, with white hair and the sharpest black eyes Diana had ever seen, sat upright facing Diana, her back quite straight, and planted her black shoes on the carpet. She then proceeded to fire question after question at the British visitor.

"And do the British appreciate that their blockade is of a free nation?" she began ominously.

"I do not think they appreciate the situation at all, Mrs. Johnson," said Diana easily, shaking her head as Mrs. Bellows would have interrupted with a tactful remark. "From the talk of London, one would think America still a colony. No, I think they do not realize at all what has gone on."

"And pray tell me, what do they think hap-

pened in seventeen seventy-six? Do they not know
we fought a war, and won it?"

Diana tried truthfully to tell her of the situation. She found herself speaking with some feeling
and more knowledge than she knew she had of the
current political situation. The ladies, to her surprise, were most knowledgeable about economic
matters, the cotton trade, sailing ships, the acts of
their Congress, and so on. They had a lively discussion over the coffee cups and plates of cakes.

"Indeed, Lady Diana, if you had been distressed, I should have stopped the conversation at
once," beamed Maria Bellows later, when the
guests had departed. "But you seemed to enjoy it,
and you certainly held up your end of the de-
bate!"

"May I compliment you and your girls on your
intelligent discussion," said Diana seriously. "In
London, our ladies do not usually discuss such
matters—only the bluestockings, of course, and
people look down their noses at them. I—I quite
like it, that ladies can discuss politics here!"

"Whyever would we not?" demanded Dora.
"Are not females permitted to have minds in England?"

"They have minds. They are not supposed to ex-
pose them in public," said Diana, with a laugh.
Then she grew thoughtful. Other women of her
acquaintance could talk of such matters, but
Diana had not felt free to do so. Her father had
severely discouraged her from taking part in political discussion. Females were made to keep a

house comfortable, welcome guests, see that food was served at proper times and temperatures.

She could not recall when her father had ever taken her into his confidence. Indeed, she had been banished to her drawing room when talk turned to serious matters of the empire. He had treated her mother in the same manner. She had found that Sir Geoffrey felt the same way, and had concluded that all men did. But perhaps it was not so.

She wondered about Jeremy McCullough. Would he banish his wife from the discussion of politics? They had not talked much of governments, rather of stars and fate, of cloudy skies and the beauty of the ship as she sailed full-masted through deep troughs of blue sea.

Dora greeted Diana one morning with a radiant smile. "There is going to be a ball, Diana!"

"Oh, really?" asked Diana, coming farther down the stairs. A ball; how she would love to dance! But of course, she would not be asked. Courteous as the Americans were to her, they could not ignore the fact that she was a prisoner.

"At the home of Mr. Prentice. He has a grand, big house, and all across the back of it is a splendid ballroom. There will be a hundred guests, Mummy says, and I am to be allowed to attend. I have an invitation." Dora was pink with excitement.

Maria Bellows came out from the kitchen, beaming. "There, now, she has told you, and I wanted to myself! Your invitation is here, my lady.

And, Dora, you are not to impose upon Lady Diana's good nature— I told you again and again how to address her ladyship!"

Mrs. Bellows mingled her scolding with a loving pat on her daughter's head. Diana accepted the white envelope with bewilderment.

"Oh, Mrs. Bellows, I have begged the girls to call me Diana," she said, examining the bold handwriting on the envelope. "Please allow them to do so. They have been so gracious and friendly, they make me feel quite comfortable."

"Well, well, all shall be as you wish," said Mrs. Bellows, a little disappointed. She seemed to enjoy saying "my lady" as frequently as possible.

Diana opened the envelope slowly, and Dora peered over her shoulder. "There it is! 'We request the pleasure of your company, Lady Diana Somerville, to a ball to be held—' Oh, isn't it glorious? It's the first time we've had a ladyship at one of our balls, and everyone is dying to meet you," she said ingenuously.

"But am I not a prisoner?" asked Diana of Mr. Bellows later in the afternoon when he returned home from his business. He smiled at her kindly. He was a warm man, not at all like her own father. She thought Mr. Bellows had a hard time remembering that all girls did not belong to his own flock, as he called them.

"Not at all, not at all. Oh, technically, of course," he added. "But pooh, who minds that? We are all happy to have you with us. You and your father, your fiancé, and Captain Talbot are all invited. We do hope you will come. There will be country dancing mostly, but also formal dances, even a waltz or two, Mrs. Bellows says." And he looked affectionately at his wife.

"I should love to come." Diana's thoughts had flown to Captain McCullough. She longed to ask if he would be there.

Jennie later answered her question without her asking it. "Captain McCullough is invited. He must come; oh, we are all simply dying to see him again!"

"Miss French is dying also," giggled Amy, with a flutter of her lashes at Diana. "Christine French is frightfully jealous of you, Lady Diana. To think of all that time you spent on board *his* ship, and she has only been aboard in harbor, when he had a party. And to have Captain McCullough's cabin! Oh, I heard from my friend Sue that Christine French went positively green when she heard!"

Jennie looked rather anxiously at Diana. "It is not as though she thought anything *wrong*," she said, concerned for Diana's feelings. "She has a feeling for Jeremy McCullough, you see. Though I am not so sure he returns it. She is very strong-willed."

"But so beautiful!" sighed Amy.

"But she has a bad temper," said Dora wisely. "He does not like her when she shows her temper. Marcia said that one time he turned on his heel and walked straight away from her!"

"What will you wear? Oh, may I ask?" Jennie said.

Three pairs of eyes fixed on Diana. "I simply don't know," she said. "I—well, I don't know what to wear. Are we to be very formal? Perhaps you would look at my gowns and advise me," she said, on an inspiration.

That suggestion met with great favor. They had watched each day what she wore, studied her bonnets with wide eyes, copied the way she tied a scarf and held her reticule. In Diana's room, Hester immediately opened the wardrobe and held out gown after gown, to a chorus of oohhs and aahhs.

"The blue satin, with the pearls," sighed Jennie. "Oh, that must be the one. It has such a gorgeous, huge skirt—"

"Is it not too formal?" asked Diana doubtfully, studying the blue satin with its high neck and long sleeves. "And it would be dreadfully hot. I never dreamed it would be so warm in Boston."

"It would be hot," said Dora. She darted over to study the gowns. "What about this one?"

The gown was one of Diana's newest. Its low neck showed off her slim shoulders, its simple lines revealed her slim form. It was in a straight Grecian mode, with a draped tunic crisscrossing the front and back of the gown. The fabric was of a cool blue silk tissue, bordered in silver with a Greek key design. With the gown, Diana wore a tall feather in her hair.

Romantic Amy leaned toward a rose satin gown edged with white swansdown. But Diana thought Dora had the most practical head and the best fashion sense of the three girls. She chose to wear the Grecian gown.

She dressed rather nervously on the night of the ball. She had seen nothing of Jeremy since she had arrived in Boston. Even her fiancé had called on her only once; he was busy trying to see every important dignitary in Boston, and had little time for her.

She had the feeling that time was running out. It was late July. Soon they would leave Boston, and she might never see Jeremy again. And Sir Geoffrey was colder than ever. She did not want him to be other than that, but how could she marry him? And how could she possibly return to the rigid formality of her life in England? The thought of the huge London town house, the receptions when everything must be perfectly arranged, the country house she had enjoyed only when she had been alone there— She shivered even in the warmth of the Boston evening.

She descended the stairs slowly. Her gown floated just above her neat ankles, which were crisscrossed with the blue ties of her slippers. She carried a silver fan of Chinese design: two ladies stepping across a little bridge. Her reticule was of blue and silver, and she thought involuntarily of that first time she had met Jeremy and been forced to powder his hair.

She was the first to come down to the Bellows' cheerful drawing room. She stood at the window and gazed out dreamily into the dusk. Would she see Jeremy tonight? Her heart beat more rapidly at the thought. She pressed her slim hand to her breast. What if he had set sail? But surely someone would have said so! Perhaps his new frigate was not ready, the one with all the guns—the one in which he would sail forth into battle once more. *Oh, Jeremy,* she thought in desolation, and trembled a little.

Dora darted into the room. "Oh, you look simply splendid!" she cried. "I adore that gown! Someday I shall wear one just like it!"

"Thank you, my dear, you are most kind." Diana smiled, and gently patted a lock of brown hair into place. Dora at fifteen was so open and sweet, awkward and earnest. She would miss her. If only she had had such a sister—but how foolish to yearn constantly for what she could not have. She realized once again how lonely her life was—no sisters, a brother who cared nothing for her, a disapproving father.

When she praised Dora's gown, the girl smiled worshipfully. The gown did suit her. Mrs. Bellows had made a shrewd choice. Dora wore a simple rose dress that set off her face with a row of ruffles. It was not too elaborate for a girl of Dora's age, yet there was nothing childish about the gown.

Jennie soon joined them, radiant in silvery-white chiffon silk. It quite transformed the practical Jennie. Diana thought she looked stunning. Amy came in, sulky in a blue gown which had not taken the iron well, she said. But she did look pretty when she smiled, and danced around, whirling her skirts.

Mrs. Bellows bustled in, pretty in rose tissue silk. Mr. Bellows followed, straightening his golden waistcoat and his formal blue coat. Now they all stood waiting for Lord Somerville, trying not to show their impatience.

He had not wished to attend; he had more important things to do, he had said to Diana. She had compressed her mouth against the wish to say she wished he would *not* come, he would only throw ice water over the proceedings. She counted on his usual good manners to cover his boredom, but could not be entirely sure of that. He felt contempt for the Americans, and often did not bother to hide it.

Lord Somerville finally appeared, looking as dour as Diana had feared he would. They finally set out in three carriages. They soon pulled up at a large white house, its windows aglow with candles. The path to the house blazed with flares, and white-gloved Negro servants handed them down courteously from their carriages.

They stepped through wide-opened doors and into a wood-paneled hallway. On either side of the hall was a large, gracious drawing room. A servant directed them to a smaller room where they left their short cloaks. Jennie squeezed Diana's hand convulsively. "*He* is here," she whispered dramatically.

"Who?" For a moment Diana thought she

meant Jeremy, and her heart seemed to stop with a jolt, then beat twice as fast.

Dora answered with a giggle. "Her beau! Jimmy Prentice!"

"Oh, Dora, don't be silly!" Jennie's face was crimson with embarrassment. "He isn't—"

"He likes you frightfully," said Dora positively.

"Oh, do you think so?" Jennie fussed with her gloves, looking unsure. Diana put an arm about her waist.

"And you told me nothing," she reproached gaily.

"We—we haven't said anything! I mean—I'm but nineteen, and he just finished law school—"

She looked happy suddenly, and beyond her Diana saw a handsome, serious-looking young man approach and bow to them. "Welcome to our home," he said, his gaze on Jennie.

Jennie, even in her fluster, remembered her manners and introduced him to Diana. Young James Prentice managed a very correct bow and a kiss on her white-gloved fingers. Then he directed the girls into the large ballroom at the back of the house.

"Oh, how lovely!" cried Diana as they entered. The room was long and wide, with polished floors, and windows thrown open to the night and the garden. Mirrors framed one wall, and tall vases filled with summer flowers stood near the entrances. But all attention was on the brilliant Chinese lanterns, lit with candles, which hung from the ceiling. The colorful lanterns cast a rose and blue and green glow over the room. "I have never seen anything quite so lovely," repeated Diana, to the satisfaction of young Mr. Prentice.

"A friend of Papa brought them from China on his latest voyage," James informed her. "And now permit me to introduce a gentleman to you, Lady Diana," and he brought forward a smiling young man.

Diana recognized the young man as the one she had met in the office of the magistrate. He asked her for the first dance, and she nodded, giving him a radiant smile.

As he drew her into the square forming in the center of the room, he said, "I trust you are happy here, Lady Diana?"

"Oh, very happy. I could not ask for a more gracious hostess than Mrs. Bellows, and her girls are so friendly and sweet. I am most grateful to Boston for allowing me to remain there."

"We must make you so happy here that you will not wish to leave us, Lady Diana!"

Diana was soon grateful for the lessons the Bellows girls had given her in the latest American dances. She was claimed for almost every dance, and sat or stood out only when she wished. She kept watching for Jeremy, but he did not appear. Perhaps he had not been invited, after all, or was out of town, or too busy.

Quadrille followed minuet, and then came a merry round dance. She was breathless and laughing as they finished. Jimmy Prentice brought her an ice, and one for Jennie, and they stood chatting at the edge of the floor near the gardens. She had noted a beautiful girl with flaming red hair and a golden silk dress which set off her enticing figure.

Then suddenly she saw Jeremy. And he was standing beside the red-haired girl, who pouted lusciously up at him.

"Oh, there is Captain McCullough!" said Jennie. "And Miss French has captured him," she went on, disappointed. A moment later the handsome couple had joined in a square with three other couples.

Christine French. How stunning she was! All were looking and murmuring as the handsome captain danced with her. Diana looked also, and felt a strange, hot anger. How could he? He had not even looked in her own direction! She felt so furious that she grew quite distressed. What was the matter with her? She had never felt like this before, not at any ball, not over any man!

"Look how jealous Marcia is!" murmured Jennie in Diana's ear.

Jealous! Yes, that was what was the matter with her, thought Diana. She felt hotly jealous of whoever was held in Jeremy's strong arms! She noted that he no longer wore the sling. He was in uniform, however, and his tall, elegant figure, shining hair, made him more striking than any other man in the room. His laughter rang out as though he were on his own quarterdeck, and all would turn and look at him.

Now he was dancing with Marcia, pretty in green and gold. Now he was with another girl, a gentle-faced blonde. Diana turned, smiled blindly at her partner, and agreed that it was terribly warm tonight, and yes, she would like another ice. He fetched it for her, and then she was standing near the windows again, chatting with the man without knowing what he said, when someone behind her touched her arm.

She knew without turning who it was. No other man had the power to thrill her. At the same moment, she saw Sir Geoffrey enter the ballroom, and languidly survey the dancers. He was late also, very late, rudely late.

"Lady Diana? This is my dance, I think!" A strong arm turned her about, and she looked up into the laughing green eyes of Jeremy McCullough.

The music was beginning, the dreamy airs of a waltz. The scandalous, sensuous waltz. The same music to which they had danced on the night they had met in London, at the home of a Russian prince. How long ago that seemed.

"I asked them to play it—for us," Jeremy murmured in her ear.

She drew back sharply. She had felt the bitter pangs of jealousy. She had not seen him for many days, and now he seemed to think he could come around and dance the waltz with her, claim her in front of everyone—

"I see my fiancé approaching," she said coldly. "I dance the waltz only with him."

His green eyes flashed, and he laughed down at her, and whirled her into his arms and onto the polished floor. Before Sir Geoffrey's astonished gaze, Jeremy danced her across the room. Most of the guests had drawn to the side. Only a few danced the waltz, and they watched with wonder, admiration, and a few with disapproval, as the sea captain danced with the British lady.

His strong hand was on her waist, his other hand clasped hers in a crushing hold. She kept her gaze lowered deliberately, so that all she saw was his white shirt front. She was conscious that he gazed down intently at her, and she knew that if she looked up, there would be laughter in his face.

She caught one glimpse of the musicians, playing in the corner on a dais. They were sawing away on their violins, the pianist pounding his instrument so earnestly that sweat rolled down his forehead. But all were grinning happily as the couples passed them.

The music slowed hauntingly, then ceased. In a darkened corner far from the musicians, Jeremy paused also, with Diana still held close to him. His head bent, and she felt his mouth pressed to her bare shoulder. Then he lifted his head and held her away from him, so that he could gaze down over her, over the blue and silver gown.

"You look—delightful—my lady," he murmured. "Thank you for the dance!"

He straightened, his mocking gaze devilish at her embarrassment. Following her gaze, he turned to see Sir Geoffrey approaching them.

"Oh, there you are, Sir Geoffrey. Any luck with your mission? Have you seen Mr. Waverly?"

Sir Geoffrey bowed formally, his gaze sternly disapproving on his fiancée. "I do not talk business at balls," he said flatly.

Jeremy laughed out loud, and left them. Sir Geoffrey took Diana's hand and raised it to his lips, but did not touch it with his mouth. "I am amazed at you, Diana," he said coldly.

Beyond him, Jeremy was striding across the floor. Would he seek out the gorgeous Christine French? No, he was bowing before Jennie Bellows, to the girl's obvious delight.

"Really?" murmured Diana, as Sir Geoffrey seemed to expect an answer. "You are very late, sir," she said, carrying the battle into his camp.

"I have been busy. I will speak of that later. I am shocked that you should dance with *him*, our jailer! And the waltz! You should not waltz in public with anyone but me!"

"You have not asked me," she said, waving her fan slowly. Hester would have been warmed by her look, but Sir Geoffrey did not know her so well.

"No flippancy, please. I have heard much of Captain McCullough's reputation with the ladies since we reached Boston. He is not a proper person for you to know. I think your father should speak to you, and the sooner we return to England, the better."

She scarcely heard him. For Jeremy was coming their way, dancing with Jennie, and facing in their direction as the quadrille approached. And he gave Diana a broad, unmistakable wink!

She started, drew herself up, and gave him a frown. His shoulders shook with laughter, then he looked down at Jennie, turned her gently about, and all Diana saw was his broad shoulders and back.

"I suppose we had best stand up for a dance or two," said Sir Geoffrey. "To show we bear no ill will toward our hosts, if we are to call them that."

He held out his arm. She put her fingers on it lightly and allowed herself to be led to the formation of another quadrille. Jeremy was in the new set, and Diana had the galling experience of watching him with the flashing-eyed Christine French as they danced the movements with practiced skill.

Diana danced again and again, sometimes with her fiancé, until he wearied of it, then with Jimmy Prentice, who filled her ears with praise of Jennie. And with other gentlemen, who insisted they had never seen such beauty, such grace, such charm, as she possessed. Was she remaining here long? Jeremy claimed her again for a set, but there was no more talk between them.

They did not go home until past two o'clock, and Dora pronounced it the finest ball she had ever attended. As she was but fifteen, she was laughed at by Amy, but Diana privately agreed with her. It was the most exciting, exasperating, beautiful ball she could remember.

Chapter 12

All the girls slept late the next day. They rose at noon, dreamy-eyed, and compared notes on the ball, to the satisfaction of everyone.

Lord Somerville joined them for a rare appearance at luncheon. "Captain McCullough asked to call upon me this afternoon," he said, interrupting the conversation at table, scarcely seeming to realize he did so.

Everyone stared at him. "Is it serious, Papa?" Diana asked finally.

"Serious?" he frowned. "It is business. However, he asked that you should join us for the conversation. I do not know why. He said he could come about three-thirty or four o'clock."

"Oh, then I shall serve tea," Maria Bellows chimed in, quite serenely avoiding Lord Somerville's glare. "We shall enjoy having him. He is such a busy man, one must snatch such moments of conversation as one can."

Mr. Bellows took pity on Lord Somerville. "You might take him into my study later on, if you wish, my lord," he offered. "Some talk away from the ladies after tea."

Later on, Lord Somerville said privately to Diana, "They are very pushing, these Americans! Imagine joining in on a private talk!"

"In their own house, Papa?" she said gently. "We are their guests, and they have not made us feel like prisoners at all, have they? I think they are most kind."

He glared at her suspiciously. "You have changed much since we left England, Diana," he said heavily. "You have become most forward, and almost—rude—for a lady so well brought up. I blush for your manners. You must learn to control yourself."

She flushed and bit her lip against angry words. Finally she managed to reply, "I am sorry if I have offended you, Father, or caused you uneasiness. I only wish to speak my mind at times, and not merely listen in silence to others' conversation."

"That is what I object to!" he said forcefully. "You know nothing of politics, nor should a female trouble herself with anything but the care of the household. Sir Geoffrey has mentioned to me that he finds you much changed, and is becoming uneasy about the match. I assured him that once we return to England, you shall be your former self, gentle and obedient like your mother."

Once we return to England! The words tolled in her mind like a death knell. Return from this gay and happy atmosphere, where Mrs. Bellows treated her almost like a daughter, and the girls like sisters she had never had.

And never to see Jeremy again! How could she endure that? She knew she would watch the gazettes for his name, for the name of his ship, watch with dread in her heart.

The wife of Sir Geoffrey would be made to repress her true feelings, her every emotion but the correct one of which he approved. And to share her bed with him— She shuddered in the warm summer air.

She went up soberly to her room to rest, and be alone for a time. She wished she might never have to leave the sanctuary of this home, that time might drift on and on and she might be free of making decisions. That she might be free to follow her heart! Oh, that asked too much of fate, she thought dispiritedly.

Hester came to her presently, her gaze keen on her mistress's face. Diana sat at the window, drinking deeply of the scents from the old-fashioned garden, the roses, the honeysuckle that climbed up to her second-floor window.

"Will you be changing your dress for tea, my lady?"

Diana turned a weary face to her. "Oh, yes, I suppose so," she said.

"*He'll* be coming. I thought maybe the pretty blue gown he admired on the ship," said Hester boldly, and was pleased when Diana blushed and nodded. She took out the blue muslin dress lovingly.

Hester's skillful fingers teased Diana's curls into order, catching them up on top of her head to fall to the neck in gentle disarray. It was one of the latest modes. The low neck of the gown revealed her white shoulders.

"And will he be coming often, my lady?" Hester

ventured to say, as Diana clasped a string of pearls about her throat.

"I might—never see him again," said Diana, in a low, husky voice. "We have to return to England, you know." Diana clipped on some pearl earrings and blindly sought for the matching ring.

"Do we now? And another trip on a nasty boat that goes back and forth like something demented?" Hester sniffed in disapproval. "And I have scarce recovered from the other trip!"

Diana smiled faintly. She had not recovered either, but for other reasons. She remembered the glow of sunsets, as she leaned against the wooden rail, and watched the reddish light gleam on deep purple waters. And a sea captain would pause beside her to point out a school of fish, or a star that peeped out just as the light was fading. No other journey would be like that one, never.

Dora dashed into the room, scarcely remembering to knock. "*He* is here!" she whispered dramatically. Her eyes fixed avidly on Diana as the girl rose from the dressing bench and took one last look at herself in the oval mirror. "Oh, you look stunning," she sighed.

"Thank you, Dora. You'll go down with me?"

"Mummy said I might," said Dora. "After all, I am fifteen!"

Arm in arm, the two girls descended the stairs. From the drawing room came the familiar rumble of a deep voice, chiming with the lighter voices of Jennie and Amy. Diana swept in, with

Dora clinging shyly to her, and Jeremy stood up at once.

Her father had not yet come. Her gaze went eagerly to Jeremy, to the wide grin, the handsome shoulders in the snugly fitting blue jacket, the length of his legs as he rose from the plush armchair. He came across to her with the swift stride she knew so well. He took her hand and raised it to his lips, and she felt the warmth of his mouth pressed to her fingers. No mere formality there; he meant to kiss her fingers! He came erect, and smiled down into her eyes.

"Lady Diana, how pleasant to see you once more. I can see you are blooming. Miss Dora, you have grown two more inches. You are a young lady already." And he grinned at the flustered girl.

Deliberately he took Diana's arm and led her to the sofa. Then he sat down across from her, and subjected her to a long, intent stare.

"Well, do you have everything you wish here? They have been good to you, these young flirts?" he asked solemnly. "They have not pestered you as to hair arrangements, and the latest fashions from London?"

Dora and Amy giggled. Mrs. Bellows said rather hastily, "Oh, they will pester Lady Diana, but she swears she does not mind at all! I have said over and over, they must not bother my lady—"

"Oh, please, Mrs. Bellows, you know how much I have enjoyed their company!" Diana broke in.

"They treat me like a cousin, and I have never been made so comfortable."

"Good, good," said Jeremy, still staring at her as though he would memorize her every feature. "I was forced to remove to the country. Mama and the girls had gone to her home, because my grandparents are not quite well. And I was a bit feverish with the wound to my shoulder. So they insisted on coddling me, and forbade me to ride until I became so disgusted that I rode back to town. Petticoat tyranny!" he said ruefully, and Dora giggled again.

So that was why he had not come! Diana felt relieved, and suddenly lighthearted. He had not been spending all his time with the beautiful Christine French.

"And how is your wound, Captain?" she asked, unfolding her fan and fanning herself lightly. Her cheeks felt very flushed, more than the heat of the room warranted. "You are recovering, I trust? The dance last night did not trouble you?"

"Oh, it troubled me, but not in the arm," he said in a low tone. "A certain lady gave me only two dances, and spent much time with a young sprig from London. That kept me awake all the night!"

She laughed lightly. "And your men?" she went on. "What of the wounded ones? Are they recovering as they should?"

The laughter was dashed from his eyes. The others were frankly listening. "Two of them are recovering in their homes. The others are in hospital. The one who lost his arm was deep in melancholy, swearing he could never go to sea again. I gave him a position at once in father's warehouse— That reminds me, I must inform Father he has a new employee! He cheered up a bit at that. Work shall be found for him that he can do about the docks, so he will not miss the sea too much."

"Oh, you are kind," she said impulsively, her blue eyes glowing. He reached out and touched her hand, and the touch burned like fire.

"He will be gratified at your concern," he said simply.

Dora was bursting with curiosity. "How did you know about the wounded, Diana? Did you see them? Were they hurt in a fight? Oh, you said nothing of that to us!"

Jeremy noticed Diana's hesitation and answered for her.

"She not only knew about the wounded, she tended to us on the deck, in danger of fire from the enemy. And she assisted the men in going below to the cabin, where she cared for their wounds and fed them. She was as good as a nurse, Eli Ulrich said, and his is high praise indeed. She made it her daily duty to tend the wounded, and but for her one might have died."

"Indeed, we had not heard. How good you are, Lady Diana," said Mrs. Bellows heartily. "You will credit, then, Captain, how good she has been to my girls, entertaining them with stories of London, telling them of fashions—"

"I knew it! She should come to my house and

fill my sisters' ears with all of that!" he said with a laugh. "I vowed to bring back news to them of the English dresses and bonnets, and I fear it has all gone out of my head. I tried to tell them bonnets were larger, but they would not believe me. You will come to see them soon, Lady Diana, when they return to Boston, and take me off the hook!"

He was inviting her to his home, to meet his sisters. Her heart was bursting with joy. "I shall be happy to meet your sisters, Captain," she said as demurely as possible.

He sensed her embarrassment and turned to Jennie. "Now, Miss Jennie, I hear talk you are troubling the mind of Mr. Prentice. And having seen you last night, I can understand why. You were a vision."

"Oh, Captain, how kind you are." The serious Jennie was wriggling with pleasure at his words. For Captain McCullough to praise her so!

Amy flirted with him with her long lashes, earning her a stern look from her mother. Captain McCullough exchanged a laughing glance with Diana. "Miss Amy, my sister Teresa asked about you, and vows you must come to her as soon as they return to Boston. She swears none but you will know all the news she wishes to hear. Now, what news would this be, that is not to be found in the gazettes?"

Amy giggled, and Dora pinched her arm teasingly. "Oh, perhaps it is about school, and our lessons this autumn," she said, when she had caught her breath.

"I warrant it is not," muttered Mrs. Bellows darkly. "More like, gossip about certain young gentlemen!"

Diana thought about the school, the young ladies' academy that the girls attended. They took their lessons seriously—she had seen some of their books on French, grammar, mathematics, history—so much more serious than the few she had used with her governess. Diana had had to seek out for herself the books she wished to study, and had struggled through them on her own, so that she might understand what her father and others were discussing.

What must it be like to attend a school where other young ladies came and went? Where they might talk and giggle between lessons, and learn to know each other well? It might have taken away some of the chill of her growing up. She knew again the pang of those cold years when no one had been close to her to confide in.

Finally Lord Somerville appeared, stately in full afternoon dress. Jeremy broke off a story he was telling to rise and greet the man. He was about to go over to Lord Somerville when that gentleman paused in the center of the room and made him a deep, formal bow. Jeremy's eyebrows shot up. He paused, and bowed deeply in return.

All merriment had fled the gathering. Diana felt downcast at her father's behavior.

"Captain McCullough, shall we adjourn to the study to talk?" asked Lord Somerville.

"Lord Somerville, your servant, sir," murmured

Jeremy. "However, it is not necessary. I merely have some papers to return to your hand directly. Also I wished to inquire as to your comfort and your plans."

Lord Somerville frowned, but finally seated himself in a straight chair.

"I will order tea to be served," Maria Bellows murmured. She rang a little bell, and the tea trolley was brought in so promptly that Diana thought the servants had probably been hanging about, waiting impatiently for the call.

When tea had been served, Jeremy reached into his capacious breast pocket and drew out some papers. He handed them to Lord Somerville. "Your papers, sir. I have returned Sir Geoffrey's as well. Of course. I should tell you they have been copied," he added thoughtfully, and picked up his teacup.

Lord Somerville's face reddened with anger. He leafed through the papers, as though suspecting some might have been taken, then reluctantly set them beside him on a table.

"Well, well, harrumph," he said. "And what is the decision, sir? Are we still prisoners?"

Dora gave a little jump and moved closer to Diana on the sofa. Jeremy's face was enigmatic.

"I really couldn't say that you are prisoners, sir. Only that you and Sir Geoffrey should not venture outside Boston without permission. I could give you advice, if you wished to listen. That is your decision, of course."

Lord Somerville shifted uncomfortably on his straight chair. He did not wish to ask advice, that was patently clear to all. But he was a diplomat, and a pragmatic one.

"If you would be so kind," he finally forced himself to say.

"Not at all. I think your mission has no chance now, none at all. Both the trade mission, and the—ah—other diplomatic mission are out of the question, now our countries are at war with each other."

"Indeed! And what do you suggest that we do? Remain here until your country is beaten, and England sends for us?"

Dora gasped, then clapped her hand over her mouth. Diana stiffened, clenching her teacup convulsively. Her father must be enraged, to so forget his manners.

"We do not intend to be licked, sir. I think you might have a very long wait," said Jeremy, his eyes flashing. He seemed to take control of himself with an effort, and a glance at Diana's set face seemed to calm him. "My suggestion is that you return to England as soon as passage can be arranged. You could ask for asylum here, but I think you will wish to be in your own country."

A long silence followed. Diana's heart had sunk. Return to England—so soon! And Jeremy himself advised it! He did not care if she remained or not, for all his kind words.

"And how do you think that can be arranged?"

her father burst out. "I dislike speaking of this before females, but dammit, our ships are not allowed to land here in Boston, and we are not allowed to leave! How do you think we can take ship to England?"

"I imagine it can be arranged," said Jeremy coldly. "You need only apply to the proper authorities. Unless, of course, you wish to remain as our guest."

Lord Somerville drew a deep breath, as though reminding himself of his status here. "You are most gracious. However, our place is in England, as you indicated. We must return as soon as possible. To whom should we apply?"

"The magistrate to whom you spoke when you arrived. At least, he is the first step. The matter must be considered, and of course they will have to contact a British ship somehow," said Jeremy thoughtfully. Then a devilish twinkle came alive in his eyes. "Of course, I have it! If you wish to speed your return without going through the authorities, I could help you arrange it."

"How is that?" asked Lord Somerville suspiciously.

"I know a chap who is a spy on a British ship. I'll get in touch with him, and he can pass the word along. We could get you out to the ship in a rowboat—"

"Indeed, sir, you choose to mock me!" said Lord Somerville, outraged. "I regret that I cannot accept such an offer." His face was full of shock at the man's brazen effrontery.

Jeremy shrugged regretfully and gave Diana a wink. She wanted to burst into laughter at the wild suggestion. Jeremy had meant what he said, that was what was so funny! He knew all kinds of men and had been a spy himself!

Lord Somerville finally excused himself. He had had enough of Captain McCullough for that day and forever, as he confided to Diana later. The man was an impudent rascal, and how he came to be in command of a ship was beyond his comprehension. He probably had acquired the position through the influence of an indulgent father. Diana did not inform her father of her own knowledge, that the ship was Jeremy's own.

But when Lord Somerville departed in cold disdain, the conversation immediately became lighter. Jeremy set out to entertain his hostess and the girls with some lighthearted stories of the sea. The more outrageous they were, the more the girls gasped. He had them in gales of laughter at a story of some pirates whom he had almost joined.

"Oh, how I should like to meet a pirate!" cried Dora, in high spirits.

"It would never do," said Jeremy solemnly. "He would probably fall madly in love with you, and reform, and then how would he earn his living? He could not remain a pirate, so he would have to become a dull sea captain. Isn't that right, Lady Diana?"

"I would not think the two occupations so incompatible," she said. Jeremy flung back his head and roared with laughter.

Dora leaned against Diana, helpless with giggles, and Diana slipped her arm about the young girl's waist. Jeremy watched them with an odd look in his eyes, a tender, wondering look. Then he turned serious and asked Diana what her plans were.

"Oh, Captain, my plans are as my father's," she said, the mischief dashed from her at once. "Where he goes, I must go."

"You might remain here. You like it here, don't you?" he asked.

They all looked at her. "I like it immensely," she said quietly, gazing steadily at her fan. "However, my home is in England."

"And you will be marrying Sir Geoffrey soon after you return," said Mrs. Bellows, with seeming innocence, but giving Jeremy a sidelong glance.

He frowned. "What of your brother?"

"He is busy about his own estate. I keep house for my father, as you know. After my—marriage, I will do the same for—Sir Geoffrey." It was oddly difficult to force the words from her throat.

"And friends?"

She shrugged. "In the diplomatic world," she said lightly, "one does not become close to anyone. It is not done, you see."

"That sounds awful for you, Diana," said Dora impulsively, hugging her waist. "You ought to stay here with us!"

"An excellent idea," said Jeremy with a smile. "However, all need not be decided today. We must persuade you to remain in Boston. By the way, Eli Ulrich asked permission to call upon you one day, and bring his wife with him."

"I shall be happy to receive him," said Diana. Soon after, Jeremy stood to take his leave.

"I have far outstayed my welcome. You are most gracious to me, Mrs. Bellows," he said.

When he had left Diana went upstairs to be alone awhile. If she only might remain in Boston a little longer. If only she might remain forever! Oh, but how could that be?

Chapter 13

Jeremy did not return. The next days passed slowly, and July turned into August. Diana wandered in the little garden, picked flowers for her hostess, and helped arrange them. She walked the cobblestoned streets with the girls, or accompanied them when they called on their friends.

And all the time, she wondered. Could she but remain in Boston for a time, Jeremy might call again. He might become serious about her. But no, there was Christine French and other females of his acquaintance. And besides, he was not the marrying kind; he loved the sea. No, there was no hope for her.

Yet—what if— And her heart would bound at the thought of his warm mouth pressed to her lips. He was not indifferent to her. His green eyes flashed to hers, he laughed at her, was tender with her. Surely that meant something?

She blew hot, blew cold. Her hopes fluctuated so wildly that it was small comfort when Mr. Bellows announced casually at dinner one evening that Captain McCullough had gone to New York City on business for his father.

Then one bright August morning, Sir Geoffrey came to call. He usually arrived in the afternoon, stayed for tea, then disappeared into the study to talk with her father. Today he asked for Diana.

Dora came racing into the garden for her. "Sir Geoffrey is here and wishes to speak with you," she said, her eyes as anxious as those of a small puppy. "Oh, he seems to be so cold, Diana! Are you sure that you love him?"

Diana hesitated, then said gently, "The marriage was arranged for me, Dora. It is settled," and she felt chilled herself, as Dora's face fell.

"Oh, it does seem too bad," murmured the girl, and gave her hand a squeeze. "Perhaps he means to return to England alone, and you will go later," she added hopefully.

Diana gave Dora her basket of flowers and went into the back hallway. She paused before a mirror to arrange her hair, brushing back some wanton curls. Sir Geoffrey disliked her to look disheveled. But her dress of white muslin was suitably demure, she decided. Then she proceeded to the drawing room, to find her fiancé pacing back and forth, a frown on his handsome face. His gray eyes were wintry as she entered the room.

He closed the door after her, bowed over her hand, and saw her to a chair. His grave formality warned her that he was preoccupied. That could only mean trouble.

"And how are you, my dear," he said, in an unusual display of interest.

"Quite well, thank you, and you?" She folded her hands in her lap, the long, well-shaped hands Dora so admired.

"Well, thank you, but uneasy, I must confess."
He sat down, hitching up his trousers and pulling
down his waistcoat. For all his irritation at the
fact that he was a prisoner, he managed to eat
well, thought Diana dispassionately. He must
have gained some ten pounds here. Or had she
never noticed before that his chin was not entirely
firm, but softened by a plumpness under it? And
his eyes were darkened with shadows from late
nights. Where had he found dissipation here?
Surely no little ballet girls, such as the ones he
adored in London? At home, gossip had kept her
informed, so much so that Sir Geoffrey would
have been shocked at the extent of her knowledge.

"I believe you have something to tell me?"

"Yes, yes. Ah, well. Passage home is being arranged—through channels," he said significantly.

For a moment, she thought wildly of Jeremy's
spy. Surely not, surely not! "Indeed, sir?" she
managed to say without a tremor.

"Indeed. I have managed to make some friends
in high places, I might inform you. Not difficult
to do. They fall all over themselves at a British title. I am convinced that many of these colonists
never wished to detach themselves from England.
I may have some good news for the king when I
return," he added complacently.

"You will probably have to give the news to the
Prince Regent," she said serenely. "The king is ru-
mored to be mad again."

"Diana! How dare you speak so of His Majesty?
And what do you know of the matter?"

"I read the gazettes in London, sir. I am neither deaf nor blind, much as you seem to think otherwise."

He sat forward in his chair to stare at her severely, then finally leaned back in displeasure. "Your father is right. The sooner we return to England, the better. Your manners and your self-control have deteriorated here in the colonies."

"You mean, in the United States of America, sir?" She could not resist one final jab, though she told herself wearily it could do no good for her cause.

He frowned, then ignored the remark. "I have discovered something about these Americans. They are sentimental and romantic," he said, with something of a sneer. "They are much intrigued that my fiancée consented to come to America with me."

"With my father, sir," she corrected. "Otherwise, it would have been improper, as you will surely admit. I do hope you have not told people that I accompanied *you?* I do not wish my reputation to be damaged."

He got up to pace about the room restlessly. A sure sign of agitation, thought Diana, watching him indifferently. How could she ever have consented to marry the man? He was a snob and a bully, for all his courage and his distinguished looks. As for his promising career as a diplomat, what did that matter to her?

Sir Geoffrey was going on: "I have conceived a plan. Since the Americans are slow in arranging our passage home, I shall give them a little push. Our case would be stronger should they be made aware of the romance of our situation."

"*Romance*, sir?" She was incredulous.

"Yes indeed." He paused to help himself to snuff, then sneezed into his linen handkerchief. Satisfied, he put away the handkerchief with decision. "I have decided that we shall be married at once, here in Boston. With much pomp and ceremony, of course. That will appeal to their romantic natures, and they will then see the need for us to have a honeymoon, a journey home to England."

She sat paralyzed, unable to speak. Marriage— to him—at once? Oh, no, no, no! cried her mind. Her lips could not open.

"I spoke to your father about it. He reluctantly agreed with me. Of course, he had set his mind to a marriage in the abbey, with the Prince Regent present. It would bring much attention to us and advance our careers, as you can imagine." He paused to contemplate that idea with pleasure, and regret. "But no, it is more important for us to leave America and return to England. So we will marry here."

"Oh, no," she whispered, but he did not seem to heed her.

He strode about the room, detailing his plans. "We can marry in a Church of England here—I have found one such. It can be arranged to take place within two weeks, I believe, according to their laws. You will need a wedding dress and veil.

There is a dressmaker—" and he went on and on.

She sat as though caught in a nightmare. Not marriage to him! Not to Sir Geoffrey! And he was cold to her, cold! To plan the wedding to include the Prince Regent, he and her father, merely to advance their careers! Oh, she could have laughed and wept.

She had known that he had asked for her because she suited him as a hostess, because her father was Lord Somerville and she was Lady Diana Somerville. And her father was sensible of Sir Geoffrey's connection to the Prince Regent, which would be advantageous to him. But what about me? Diana cried inside herself. What about me? Am I to be crushed between the two of them? Her hands clenched at each other desperately.

Sir Geoffrey sat down again and looked at her expectantly. "Well, what about it?" he asked sharply.

"No," she said.

"*No?*" He was outraged. "How ridiculous, Diana. I have told you it is necessary—"

"No," she said, more firmly. "I—I am not ready to marry yet. You said—Father said—when we returned to England, then we would begin— Besides, he said six months— It is not yet three—"

"But I have told you why it is necessary now," he said, with quiet exasperation. "Listen, Diana, I will explain it to you again."

"No, don't bother, I heard you the first time," she said wildly, springing up. He rose also and followed her stupidly as she paced about the room.

She went over to the window, he followed; she went to the mantel, he followed, gesturing and arguing as vociferously as though he were in the House of Lords.

"The Americans are chivalrous and romantic. If we give them a splendid wedding, a really magnificent show, with gown, bridesmaids—you can enlist the Bellows girls, I presume, or I shall find someone of more breeding—flowers, a great reception in one of their government halls—"

"No," she finally managed to interrupt him, "I do not wish to marry you—now." She strangled on the last word. She did not wish to marry him—ever.

His voice became gentler, as though he sensed some panic in her, and must be cautious. "Diana, I know this is hasty. I would not have it so, believe me! A female wishes all her friends about her at this time, and you would have your brother, also, in England. However, much as I appreciate your point of view—"

He had never appreciated her point of view, never even listened to it before this, thought Diana, clenching her fists in unconscious dismay. If he never listened to her now, how would it be after marriage?

"You have promised to marry me," said Sir Geoffrey, catching her small hands in his big ones. "You know I shall adore and cherish you forever."

She knew nothing of the sort. He used words like this only when it suited him. She drew her hands away gently, and seated herself again. She must be cool and calm, or he would overwhelm her with his arguments.

"I did not promise to marry you in such a short time, Sir Geoffrey," she said sternly. "I am not ready, my bride clothes are not ready. I do not wish to marry in haste— I see no reason for such haste."

He stared at her in exasperation. Just then her father tapped at the door, opened it, and came in.

"All settled?" he inquired briskly. "What is the date?"

"I am not going to marry Sir Geoffrey. In America," Diana hastily amended.

"Not going to marry—" Her father stared at her, then at Sir Geoffrey, who shook his head and went over to the window to stare out gloomily. "But, Diana, surely he has explained to you how necessary this is. A splendid plan, really, a diplomatic coup—"

Diana did not trouble to hide her outrage. "I shall not marry to produce a diplomatic coup, Father!" She stood up and went to the door. She was shaking with rage—and fear. "I bid you good day, Sir Geoffrey—and wish you luck with your other diplomatic coups! Perhaps with men—and their peculiar logic—you might succeed! You do not convince me!"

And she stormed upstairs, to the amazement of the maids and Mrs. Bellows, who peered out timidly from her drawing room.

In her bedroom, she flung herself down on a chair. She drew deep breaths to control herself.

To marry so soon, and for such a reason! She would not go through with it! For a wild moment, she thought of Jeremy coming to her rescue with a brilliant plan, like the way he had slipped away from the British frigate in the fog. If only he could rescue her so! To slip away, and never have to see Sir Geoffrey again!

Hester came in presently and murmured, "Your father wishes to see you, my lady. He is in your sitting room."

Diana tightened her lips. She did not wish to see him while she was still so enraged. But she must see him sooner or later, and she did not wish to cause trouble here in the home of the kind hostess who had taken them in.

"Very well." She got up and went over to the dressing table. She powdered her reddened eyelids, brushed her hair, looked critically at herself, and finally left the bedroom.

Her father was pacing up and down the pretty room, which was far too small to provide him much relief.

"Pray, be seated," she said formally, and sat down on a straight-backed Queen Anne chair made of shining rosewood and satin. He took a matching chair, then fixed her with an unusually diffident look.

"Diana," he said soberly, "I have had a long talk with your fiancé. He feels you are timid about marriage. I have told him your mother was the same way. Ah—let a father talk to you about this."

She sighed a little. If he was going to take a kind and thoughtful approach, it would be harder to fight them both. And what weapons did she have to fight with? She could not remain in America alone and friendless. She could scarcely make a living, and had no money of her own. Her father was going to give her a dowry, but only when she married. If only she could make her own living!

Her father was going on in a soft and reasonable tone. "Geoffrey is concerned that you may think him neglectful of you. He was going to explain about that when you dashed from the room. Rather rude, you know, Diana. After all he is a relative of the Prince Regent. And a lady never dashes from the room, no matter what the provocation."

"No, Father," she murmured tonelessly.

"Geoffrey has been extremely busy on our behalf, Diana, seeing various persons of importance about Boston. He hoped to speed the very slow workings of their government, to give us release to return home. And you do want to return home to England soon, don't you?"

"I don't know," she said rebelliously.

He ignored that. "I realize that a girl wishes to have her friends about her when she marries—"

What friends? she thought. Only the polite ladies, the curious ones, who would watch her in church to see if the Prince Regent kissed her hand, or Sir Geoffrey was properly attentive. And her brother could care less about her.

"And you have always wished for a magnificent

wedding, which I have promised you. A gown
from the best French designer, a wedding veil of
Brussels lace—"

As though that mattered!

"And I did promise you a rich trousseau." He
looked pained for a moment. "I still shall give you
that, although you already have a magnificent
wardrobe which I gave you just prior to our leaving England. And the jewels, you shall have all
your mother's jewels. Geoffrey is also promising to
give you a set of diamonds, with a tiara to match.
Did you know that?" He looked encouragingly at
her, as at a child promised a doll.

She was silent, pressing her hands together in a
painful grip. Oh, if only she might remain here,
and forget Sir Geoffrey! If only she could earn her
own living. Perhaps Mrs. Bellows would know of
some position. She might teach in the school for
girls that Dora and the others attended.

Her father went on and on, pleadingly. "When
you return to London with Geoffrey, I am sure he
will arrange a splendid reception to make up for
the paltry one here. And it will be quite romantic,
don't you think? I know you used to read the ro-
mances when you were a girl. Everyone in England
will think what a romantic marriage this is."

Not when they saw how quickly Sir Geoffrey
returned to his pretty ballet girls, thought Diana,
and wished she had the nerve to voice her thought.
But it would do no good: men were expected to
entertain themselves with women other than their

wives. Her father would only think her guilty of jealousy and naiveté.

"I don't see," she said finally, when he paused expectantly, "what difference it can possibly make to the Americans, whether we have our wedding here or not. They are not close to us, scarcely know us, in fact. What difference—"

Lord Somerville brightened. Ah, the girl was going to give some rational thought to this. "You see," he said eagerly, "this is the brilliance of the plan. The Americans are very romantic. I myself have been asked by several gentlemen if it is true that you are engaged to Geoffrey. I told them, yes, that you plan to marry soon. Don't you see, they are intrigued?"

"I don't know why," she said flatly.

"Because they like a romantic story," he repeated patiently. "A beautiful girl captured by a privateer, forced to endure a long voyage on a Yankee brig—"

Her thoughts drifted off to that Yankee brig, and the captain of it. Oh, if only Jeremy were about, so she might ask his advice. But what did he care? He had shown no signs of loving her, only of wishing to engage in a light flirtation.

"It was a capital idea of Geoffrey's!" Lord Somerville was saying. "The Americans are hesitant about letting us go, but this could be the jolt they need. They would allow us to leave, on this romantic note. And what a splendid idea to carry back with us to England. Two nations at war, but all stops to celebrate the marriage of the handsome English couple! Don't you see, Diana? It could help soften relations between our nations. A great diplomatic coup!"

She hardened again. "I dislike that expression exceedingly," she said coldly. "Indeed, I find it repulsive!"

Lord Somerville looked at her as though he longed to shake her and shut her in her room as he had done when she was a child.

"Well, well, Geoffrey will come again tomorrow," he said lightly. "You will think it over, Diana. Remember, we are in your hands. He must obtain the license at once, and of course you must find a dressmaker for your wedding gown. Of lace, Diana," he said appealingly. "And pearls!"

He stood up.

"Think it over," he added, to her unresponsive face.

"I will—think it over, Papa," she said dully.

He went to the door, then turned to add one final, impressive touch. "Remember, daughter, that Geoffrey does have influence. He has the Prince Regent's ear at court. We can return in triumph—or disgrace!"

He shut the door gently behind him, proud of the tactful way he had handled this delicate situation.

Diana sat as though turned to stone. Her mind was blank. And only this morning she had walked in the garden and thought of Jeremy and wished he might come home to Boston quite soon. He had

promised to introduce her to his sisters. She would
see him again, and he would laugh and tease her
once more.

Only two hours ago, her heart had been light
and hopeful. Now—now—she felt caught in a terrible trap. Yes, she had promised to marry Sir Geoffrey. But now that that time had come close, too
close, she was terrified.

She remembered her mother, growing thin and
pale and distant. Coming nights to brush her lips
against Diana's hair as the girl lay in bed, whispering her wishes for a happy sleep. Then moving
away, her gown shimmering in the candlelight,
making her face ghostly.

She remembered the bitter arguments between
her father and mother, arguments that became
less and less frequent, until finally there was
scarcely any conversation between them at all.
Her mother sitting at the end of the table, smiling
at her guests, rouge on her cheeks, her eyes blank.
The longer absences from home, as her parents
lived the gay life in London, and Diana remained
in the country with a nurse or governess. Coldness, coldness, until the final cold, when her
mother lay dead, and Diana had touched her face
for the last time, and felt the chill creeping into
her young heart.

She pressed her hands to her own face now, her
eyes shut. She knew how it would be. No one to
know or understand or even care how she felt. Sir
Geoffrey going his way and Diana hers—after she
had produced an heir for him, of course.

She shuddered violently. That would be the worst of all. A child, a symbol of the mockery of their marriage.

"Oh, how can I endure it?" she whispered against her hands. She had caught a glimpse these past weeks of a warm, happy home. And it had made her feel like a hungry child, face pressed against the window, watching the brightness inside as the people there feasted gaily on food she had never tasted.

Chapter 14

Diana slept little that night. She lay in the great four-poster bed, gazing out at the starry night, smelling the night scents of tobacco flower and honeysuckle. Soon she would be returning to England on a British ship, the wife of Sir Geoffrey Loring. And he would share her cabin, and her bed.

She closed her eyes tightly. But sleep would not come. Her mind went round and round, desperately, and like an animal in a trap, she could see no way out.

Other girls her age with no money became governesses, or made as good a marriage as possible. There was no other way for them to live. No matter how good her mind, how much education she had, there was nothing else for her to do; she had gone over and over the possibilities. Two years ago she had tried to rebel, had discussed the idea of teaching in a school for girls, with several people she imagined might have some influence. Her father had been outraged, had forbidden it. And he had every right under the law.

Then he had turned kinder, had bought her pretty clothes, given her a grand debut in London. He had distracted her with beaux, jewels, concerts, her own carriage.

Then he had sprung the trap. Before she knew it, he had consented to her marriage to Sir Geoffrey. She had felt a little dazzled at the idea of being wife to such a man, his hostess, a power in society.

But now—now— Oh, she would give anything to exchange places with young Jennie, or even her mother! To be Maria Bellows, beloved wife of plain Nathaniel Bellows, with three charming daughters who obviously adored their mother and father. To be laughing over the luncheon table, with merry jests and loving looks. To dress up occasionally, to be escorted to a party by a man who was considerate and kind and respected—and loved.

Yes, to love, as they did in this family. That was what Diana wanted desperately—and would not have. Oh, she might come to love a child she had with Geoffrey. Yet, would she not be in the same position as her mother had been, dragged from her child, forced to neglect the child in order to play hostess for her husband? She remembered the house parties when she scarcely saw her own mother for weeks on end. The times when they went to London for the season, and she did not see her mother for months. She shuddered. She did not want that for her own child, oh, no, not to repeat such a bleak history.

What would happen if she did rebel and remain in America by herself? Could she earn her living in a school for girls? She might, although the prospect no longer seemed nearly as appealing as it had two years ago. Besides, her father would not permit it. He was her guardian until she married; that was the law. He would drag her back to England with him, in disgrace, and let her know the full weight of his displeasure, until she gave in and married at his will.

And people would know what she had done, and mock her behind their hands, and snigger at her. She flinched. She could not endure to be mocked. Society could be so cruel. They would never let her forget her brief rebellion.

Her father was eager to be promoted. If he did well in this assignment, he might come closer to the prized circle that surrounded the Prince Regent. And eventually that would mean coming closer to the throne, when the mad King George III finally died. Some said that might be soon, he was so ill at times. Her father might become a minister of state, and Sir Geoffrey would follow in his footsteps. He was already an adviser to Castlereagh.

What did a foolish woman know about such matters? she thought, punching her pillow viciously. All she would need to do was smile and simper and listen reverently to whatever they said. Only inside, she would die, slowly, painfully.

She might form her own circle in London. Some bluestockings held salons, like the Frenchwomen did, and invited learned wits and entertaining lecturers. She might improve her mind, and become famous, and people would seek her company, and her husband might come to respect her.

She flinched. That was not what she wanted. She wanted a baby in her arms, children growing up about her skirts. To be wanted and needed.

Only yesterday, Dora had gone running to her mother in tears. Mrs. Bellows had gathered her up in her arms, soothed, and comforted her. And Dora had returned later, happily, her troubles solved. Something trivial about not being invited to the party of a so-called friend. Mrs. Bellows had convinced her that it was not worth the crying over, and she should attend a party Amy was giving instead.

"After all, darling, you have a very mature mind," said Mrs. Bellows, and Dora had quoted her radiantly. And Amy had nodded, and agreed earnestly.

"You must come to my party, Dora. Do you know, Ted asked about you only the other day. He could not believe you were just fifteen. He thought we might be twins," said the flighty Amy, with unexpected understanding of her younger sister's nature.

All loving and kind to each other. What must it be like to live in a family like that? Diana finally went to sleep on the thought. But she wakened early, and lay in bed for a time. When she finally rose, she was pale from the long, wakeful night.

Hester brought her tea in bed and looked with compassion on her mistress's drawn face. She laid out the blue muslin gown that Jeremy had so admired.

"Not that one," said Diana sharply.

Hester nodded, and brought out a pale rose muslin. That would give Diana some color.

While Diana dressed in silence, she was thinking. It was all very well to dream, but the time came when one must put away dreams and face reality. And reality was her father's career, her promise to marry Sir Geoffrey, and the inescapability of that future. She owed her father obedience and respect. And much as she loved Jeremy, she could not chase after him: he had shown no signs of returning her tender emotions. It was hopeless. She might as well give in with grace.

She had breakfast on a tray in her room. She could not face the others this morning. She was sitting in the window, looking out at the garden, when Hester returned.

"Sir Geoffrey is in the drawing room, my lady. He asks if you will come down now."

Diana nodded and got up slowly. She felt stiff and worn, as though she had aged in the night. She went downstairs, saw Mrs. Bellows in the hallway, and managed a smile and "Good morning."

"Good morning, my lady," said Mrs. Bellows, surveying her anxiously. "Are you feeling all right, my dear?"

"Yes, thank you." She pressed the woman's hand and went on to the drawing room.

Sir Geoffrey was pacing the room. He, too, looked at her anxiously as she came in. He came to meet her and raised her hand to his lips.

"You look tired, my dear," he said with unusual consideration. "I feel you have not slept."

"I am quite all right, thank you." She seated herself.

He reached into his pocket and drew out a small jewel box. "I had meant to give you this yesterday, Diana," he said gently. "I fear I was so full of my own concerns, I gave no thought to yours. Will you allow me to place this ring on your hand?"

It was a splendid diamond in a gold setting. She held out her hand numbly, and he set the ring on her finger, and kissed her hand once again.

Then he seated himself quite close to her, still retaining her hand. "Diana, yesterday I was clumsy," he said earnestly. "How could I have been so remiss! I said nothing of my own feelings for you. You must have thought me very cold and selfish."

She was silent, not wishing to agree with him, and considerably surprised. He went on, after a glance at her pale face.

"You know that I have always had a strong affection for you. I have looked forward to making you my wife, the mistress of my home, which you will grace with your elegance and ease of manner. No man is more envied in England than I am, to have won your hand. The Prince Regent himself spoke of it to me before we left England. 'Sir Geoffrey,' he said, 'you are to be greatly envied!' He called you the epitome of gracious English womanhood."

"He is most kind," she managed in a choked voice.

He gave her hand an encouraging squeeze. She wondered if this was a sample of his diplomatic manner, or if he truly felt some tender emotion for her.

"I realize to some extent what you must be thinking. We are in a strange, almost savage land, much different from our London. You naturally wish to be married from the Abbey, with all its pomp and history. I have been foolish to insist on a marriage here. It would have smoothed our way, it is true. But I should not deny you the privilege of your rank. You have looked forward to an engagement with many parties and dinners, a long courtship to be shared with your friends."

She stirred uneasily. She wanted to deny this vehemently, but what other excuse could she offer for her reluctance? It was much more difficult to fight him this way then when he was cold and dictatorial.

Sir Geoffrey sensed his success, and pressed it, like the skillful courtier he was.

"Your father is much concerned about your emotions in the matter. He is right to be so. You are his only daughter, and he has discussed you with me, wishing that you should always be happy. I am most honored that he should have entrusted you to me, for he has much regard for you. You much resemble your mother, and everyone knows how he adored her. He would not allow her to stir from his side. And after losing her, he never thought of marrying any other female."

She felt some distaste at his discussion of the

subject. Yet, perhaps he had a point. She had resented her mother's long absences. Was it possible her father had thought less of the child than of his wish to keep his wife with him?

"Yes, when we are once again in England, I shall feel the same way, Diana," he said in a low, intimate tone, pressing her fingers significantly. "I confess that on the ship I was even jealous of that boor, the captain! You showed such interest in him. However, I know it was but a passing fancy, that you have not forgotten me or your promise to marry me."

She stirred and managed to wrench her fingers from his. He was watching her face keenly, his eyes narrowed, those gray eyes that saw too much.

"I have not forgotten my promise, Sir Geoffrey," she said dully.

"It would smooth matters much if we could be married here within a couple of weeks. However, I comprehend your reluctance to give up a ceremony in the Abbey, with all the attendant publicity—"

"I don't regret that at all," she said, too quickly.

He slid the trap neatly shut. "Then you do not mind marrying here? I should be so happy if you would be my wife soon, Diana. I have longed to have you for myself," he added softly. "The family jewels will look splendid on you, the diamond tiara on your beautiful hair, the bracelets on your delicate wrist." And he picked up her hand, and kissed the inside of her wrist.

She did not feel distaste; she felt nothing. Only apathy. Sir Geoffrey continued rapidly.

"I feel sure the marriage will enable us to leave America much more quickly, and your father and I can return to our duties. You are fond of some of the Americans. With our knowledge, we might be able to settle the war more quickly. Everyone admits it should never have been declared—no one here in Boston is in favor of it. What a splendid thing, if our marriage could bring about peace between our nations—or help to do so."

Of course, she thought bitterly, it would be marvelous if a marriage helped end a war. She saw little chance of its having any effect at all on the issues—the British impressment of American seamen, the trade barriers, the blockades. Did Geoffrey believe her to be so naive? Or was he so excited by the prospect of his "coup" that he actually believed this nonsense?

"And so we will be married right away," he concluded, and she realized he had been talking while her mind drifted.

She nodded. There was nothing else she could do.

"Splendid!" he said with a sigh of relief and a glance at her averted face. "I knew you would see reason. Not many women are logical, Diana, but you are. Inherited it from your father, I expect," he finished cheerfully.

They spoke of wedding plans. He knew of a clever French dressmaker in Boston. She wondered how he had heard of her— Perhaps he *had* acquired lady friends already.

When her father came in, she was ready with a smile and pleasant words, to his great relief.

"I must tell our host. I promised him I would have a great announcement for him this afternoon," said Lord Somerville genially. His daughter generally saw things his way—eventually. It only took a bit of persuasion. His words to his future son-in-law had not gone amiss. Women needed some attention paid to them, a few kisses, flattery. Sir Geoffrey had seen the point at once.

Sir Geoffrey was invited to remain for dinner that evening. He and Diana had discussed plans much of the afternoon, then her father had brought up the subject of which officials were likeliest to expedite their departure to England. Diana had slipped away to her room when she was sure they no longer noticed her.

She found Hester there, and knew she must tell her the news. "I have agreed to marry Sir Geoffrey in two weeks, Hester. I wished you to know first."

The woman gazed at her compassionately. "Yes, my lady. May I extend my best wishes for your happiness, now and ever?"

"Thank you, Hester." Diana felt a lump rise in her throat, and turned abruptly to the wardrobe. "I suppose I must wear something splendid for dinner."

Hester bit her lip against the angry protests she wished to voice: that would only make the situation worse for her mistress. So she quietly took out several gowns, and they decided on an oyster satin embroidered with pearls. Almost like a wedding gown, Diana thought bitterly. Its severe style and stand-up collar gave her a mature look, and when she added a strand of pearls with a magnificent diamond clasp, and several pearl pins in her coronet of hair, she knew she looked as elegant as any lady at court.

"Oh, how grand you look tonight, Diana!" exclaimed Dora, when the Bellows girls joined Diana in her room. "Is something special going on?"

The girl did not miss much, thought Diana. She managed a smile. "Yes, I wanted you girls to know at once. My—my father will announce tonight that Sir Geoffrey—and I—will be married in two weeks."

Amy went into raptures, Jennie concealed her astonishment and offered her sincere best wishes. Dora stared at her new friend with wide, astonished eyes.

"But I thought— Oh, Diana," she said mournfully. "You—you are really going to marry him?"

"Yes, of course," said Diana firmly. "And I should like so much for your mother to consent to your being my attendants at the wedding. Do you think she will agree?"

That distracted the girls successfully. They were bubbling over with the excitement of it as they went to the drawing room. Mrs. Bellows was bewildered, then flustered as she took in what it would mean. Her girls, to attend Lady Diana Somerville at her wedding to a British diplomat! Good gracious!

The evening passed pleasantly. Sir Geoffrey left early, to further his plans, he said, kissing his fiancée on the cheek as he departed. Lord Somerville buried himself in a local gazette, from which snorts of disapproval occasionally emerged. Mr. and Mrs. Bellows conferred with Diana and the girls about the wedding. If only she were marrying a man she could love and respect, thought Diana miserably, how happy she would be. This family was so gracious, so generous in joining in with her plans.

Sir Geoffrey called on Diana the next morning, and took her out with Jennie as chaperone. The other girl was happy at the prospect of an excursion, but silent from awe of Sir Geoffrey. They called on the French dressmaker, who promised to drop everything and come to the home of Nathaniel Bellows the very next day to take measurements. Yes, she would bring patterns and samples of fabrics. What colors did Lady Diana prefer?

Then they called on an Army officer and his wife, with whom Geoffrey had become somewhat acquainted. Diana found the couple rather stiff but pleasant enough. The officer gladly consented to stand up with Sir Geoffrey, and his wife offered to help with the reception.

As they drove past the church where the wedding would take place, Sir Geoffrey looked at it critically, and said he would examine it more closely in a few days. "Hardly the Abbey," he said, with a sigh of regret.

Later, he told Diana privately that word had gone discreetly to the magistrate who had interviewed them, that the wedding would take place soon. "I am sure it will speed our cause," he said with confidence. "I shall send him an invitation to the wedding. Doesn't hurt to have friends in high places, eh?"

She managed to smile and nod, though she felt frozen inside. Surely this was a nightmare that would pass, and she would wake to find herself in her bed, shaking with fright, the dream mercifully over. But it did not happen. She went on moving, speaking, smiling, agreeing, until she thought she would scream.

The French dressmaker called with two young assistants. All the Bellows girls were present, taking a lively part in the talk, and Mrs. Bellows was indulgent with them.

"Now, now, Jennie dear, you must let Lady Diana decide on the colors of your dresses! It is her wedding."

Diana smiled. "What color do you like, Jennie?"

"Oh, this pale lilac, Diana, is it not exquisite?" She held up the lilac silk sample longingly.

"Indeed, and it will suit your coloring beautifully. I can see it with a round neckline, and tiny sleeves, and—"

"Marvelous, marvelous," murmured the French-woman, diving into her patterns energetically. She held up a picture. "This one, Lady Diana?"

They gathered about, and finally it was decided to have the dresses made identically, but with different colors of silk. Jennie was to be in lilac, Amy in silvery blue, Dora in palest rose. Diana's dress was to be in ivory satin, with a long train, and a low neck to show off her long strand of pearls and diamonds.

Then the dressmaker showed her some samples of lace. With coldness in her heart, Diana chose a floor-length wedding veil of spiderweb Brussels lace to drape over her gown. What did it matter? She would be a beautiful bride, but what did she care?

There was a little argument about who should pay for the gowns. Diana insisted that her father should pay for them all. It was the least he could do, she thought bitterly. And he would not have to buy her a trousseau in London; by then her husband would be paying all her bills.

The chatter about gowns and veils, slippers to match, fans to carry, occupied them much of the days. There were fittings, and the gowns took shape. It all seemed to be happening to someone else. With a fixed smile on her lips, Diana went through the days. She was frozen with apprehension and despair. She not only did not love Sir Geoffrey, she despised him. He was using her for his own purposes, and he would go on using her, as her father had used her delicate mother, until the woman died.

And she loved Jeremy. She thought of him longingly, wished he would return soon. If only she might talk to him! But the days went on and still he did not return to Boston.

It was fate, she decided, lying sleepless one night. Jeremy would not return, he did not care about her, and one day soon—in only a week!—she would wake up in bed—and not be alone. Sir Geoffrey would be there, insisting on his marital rights. Long enough to get an heir, she thought.

Her face grew thinner, and the color had left it. She put on a small amount of rouge each day to cover the pallor. She knew she was not looking well, but what did it matter how she looked, how she lived?

She felt as though she were going relentlessly toward her doom. And only Dora seemed to understand how she felt. Occasionally, the girl slipped her hand into Diana's and gave it a squeeze, and when Sir Geoffrey came to call on her and made political conversation with her father, ignoring Diana most of the evening, Dora sat beside her protectively, as though to ward off his coldness.

One day soon, even Dora would not be there, thought Diana. And somehow she must keep up a bright facade of chatter, gossip, sweetness to the world, so that none would suspect anything was wrong with her marriage. It was expected of her.

She must be her father's daughter, a hostess trained to the fingertips, her hands glittering with jewels, her mouth rouged and smiling, envied, written about in the gazettes, always present at the best occasions. It was for this she had been raised.

Chapter 15

It was a warm Saturday in mid-August, four days before the wedding. Diana was hot even in a cool white muslin gown. She was sure a storm must be brewing.

A haze hung over the town and out to sea. The masts of the ships seemed to hang limply. She could see the tops of them from her bedroom window. Perhaps Jeremy's ship was out there. He might be moving somewhere about Boston, cheerful, uncaring—or perhaps calling on Christine French, laughing with her. Forgetting the British girl he had laughed with on the deck of his brig.

Forgetting his kisses on her mouth, the clasp of his hard arm about her waist. She touched her lips with her fingers. She hated it when Geoffrey tried to kiss her; she kept turning her cheek to him, and he would frown. But she could not bear to have anyone but Jeremy kiss her— Oh, what good did it do to brood? She might never see him again.

Mrs. Bellows fanned herself languidly at the breakfast table. "Dear me, it is so hot. I do hope the storm breaks and it is cooler for your wedding, dear Lady Diana. I have known brides to faint at their weddings in August."

Dora gave Diana a quick look, then turned away.

The dresses were finished and hung in a wardrobe to await the day. Sir Geoffrey would call this morning with information about their plans to leave. He had had word yesterday that approval might be forthcoming.

Diana finished her tea thirstily, but could eat nothing. She waited politely for the others, then with Dora went out to the garden to cut some flowers. Dora chattered, expecting no answers.

"Oh, isn't it hot? I remember one summer we removed to the country, it was so warm in Boston. I fainted in church, and Mama said—"

Diana clipped some white roses and some delicate tea roses, admiring the color in a detached fashion. Perhaps she might grow more roses in their English garden—but no, she would be with Sir Geoffrey. She had not seen his country manor house. Perhaps the gardens were kept by gardeners who would not allow her to interfere much. Her new home. So much to adjust to, when they returned to England. So much. A whole new life, a terrifying new life.

Sir Geoffrey came punctually at ten o'clock. Diana awaited him in the cool drawing room where the shades were still drawn against the day's sun. He bent to kiss her cheek. She accepted that and moved away gracefully, not hurriedly. He frowned after her, then seated her in a chair.

"Well, good news, my dear," he began jovially. "I believe we are making progress. I called on the magistrate yesterday afternoon, and he has half-promised that a British ship might come into harbor for us. It seems that he has made contact with a frigate blockading Boston harbor—"

A frigate. Jeremy's next ship would be a large frigate, some thirty guns, and he would go out and fight in it, laughing and happy at the action. Forgetting her. She was forgotten already.

Diana smiled and made appropriate answers.

"And you are all packed? I have spoken for rooms with a friend of mine. We shall remove there after the wedding. I might arrange for some of your trunks to be taken over on Monday."

"Hester—has begun to pack—but there is much yet to do." She thought of a wardrobe where her clothes would hang, and he would look over them, and choose the dress that she would wear that day, and command what jewels would go with it. And rule her life—and her.

The doorbell chimed. Diana heard the brisk steps of the young butler going to answer. She gazed out the window toward the gardens, half-listening as her fiancé went on.

"On Monday, I shall also speak to Mr. Humphrey about a load of tobacco to take back to England with us. I am sure a frigate would have room for it. They have excellent tobacco here in the port, up from Charleston, I found out the other day. I have bid on it, and have some hope of taking it back with us—"

A figure loomed in the doorway. Diana turned around languidly—the heat made it impossible to

move quickly. The man came farther into the
room and paused. Now she saw him, and she
clung to the arms of her chair. "Jeremy," she said
faintly.

"Lady Diana! I just returned to Boston last
night!" He hastened over to her, took her limp
hand in his, and raised it to his lips. He looked
sharply at her. "You are not well?"

Sir Geoffrey loomed over them disapprovingly.
"My fiancée is quite well, and her well-being is
not your concern, Captain McCullough!"

"Indeed, it is! I am concerned over all my prisoners," Jeremy grinned as he straightened up to
face the man.

Sir Geoffrey's face reddened with anger. "Not
much longer, sir! We plan to leave Boston quite
soon, with the permission of the authorities!"

Jeremy's smile disappeared. "Indeed? And how
do you plan to do that? No British ships are permitted in our harbor."

"Not without special cause," said Sir Geoffrey,
and grinned complacently. He drew out his snuffbox and took a pinch.

Jeremy looked down at Diana. "You have been
ill? Your face, your eyes—you do not look well, my
lady."

"I am—quite well, thank you." Her blood was
racing as she looked at him once more. She longed
to reach out and touch him, to assure herself that
he was there.

"You are back in time for our wedding, Captain," Geoffrey interrupted.

Jeremy started. "Wedding? What madness is this? You do not plan to marry here."

Sir Geoffrey gave him a bland look. "Of course we do. Why should we wait until we return to England? We marry on Wednesday next. We must send you an invitation, must we not, dearest?"

Jeremy looked at Diana. She nodded weakly. "We—marry on Wednesday. Father—wishes it, before we depart," she managed to say. She moved her left hand, and the diamond glittered.

"You cannot marry him!"

For a moment, Diana thought she had imagined the words from Jeremy's tight lips. Then she saw the blaze of his green eyes. She tried to stand, but her knees went weak. She pushed herself up from the chair.

Sir Geoffrey turned on Jeremy; the men stood only two feet apart. "You forget yourself, Captain! You have no jurisdiction over us!"

"You will not marry Diana!"

The Englishman caught his breath in fury. "You are mad! She is my fiancée, and we are to be married on Wednesday—you have nothing to say about it!"

"Oh, no?"

Jeremy struck Sir Geoffrey with his fist. The man was knocked back, staggered in his smart high boots, then recovered. Instinctively he fought back, and planted a facer on Jeremy. A red welt rose at once on the bronzed cheek. Jeremy went after him like a fighter who scents a good one.

Mrs. Bellows, who was passing along the hallway, poked her bonneted head inside, her wide eyes taking in what was happening in her best parlor. "Dear me—gracious—oh, Captain—"

Neither man paid her any attention. Diana scrambled out of the way as Sir Geoffrey half fell over the chair she was standing behind. She stood with her back to the wall, and felt her heart thump-thumping.

Jeremy gave a last blow. He drew back his arm and struck Sir Geoffrey a mighty blow on the cheek. The crack echoed through the room. The Britisher swayed, then fell like a great tree, slowly, to the floor of the pretty French carpet.

Jeremy stared down at him, massaging his bloody fist with the fingers of his left hand. His face blazed with fury. His opponent lay limply, out cold.

Then Jeremy flung around to turn on Diana. Diana would have backed up to escape him, but she was flat against the wall.

Jeremy strode to her. "You agreed to this farce? You agreed to marry that cold, calculating bastard?"

Mrs. Bellows quavered, "Dear me, Captain, this will never do. If only Mr. Bellows was home—I should call him—dear me— Captain McCullough, you should not have done that—he is our guest—"

"Did you agree?" demanded Jeremy.

"Yes," croaked Diana, nodding her head like a puppet.

"The devil you did!"

He glared down at her. She stared up at him,

fascinated, her blue gaze caught in the green fire of his eyes.

"And you looking like a kitten left out in the storm," he said, suddenly gentle. "Diana, come with me, and we'll talk about it. There's a way out of this coil—"

But she was frightened of him. She had dreamed of him, thought of him coming to her, softly, courteously offering to help. But not like this, a brute of a man, his chest still heaving with his effort, blood streaming from a cut on his face, his hand bruised and battered.

She shook her head. "No—Captain—please—"

The softness left him. "By God, you will!"

He leaned over, lifted her as though she were a child, and carried her to the door. Mrs. Bellows stumbled out of their way. In the hallway, he barked at the startled butler, "Open that door!"

The butler jerked to obey, and the doors were flung open to the sunlight. Jeremy carried Diana out into the stifling heat of the day, out past the neat hedges and trim brick walk, to his carriage. He dumped her into the seat. She tried to sit up.

"Sit still! You'll frighten the horses!" he yelped at her. And he swung up beside her, pressed her back into the seat, took up the reins, and yelled at the horses. They were off at a gallop.

Mrs. Bellows stood at the door, calling, "Oh, Lady Diana, shall I tell your father?"

"Tell him I'm going to marry his daughter," Jeremy yelled back at her. "Sooner or later!"

A passerby looked up curiously at the two and

began to laugh. Diana turned on Jeremy, humili-
ated, stunned. "You are making me the laughing-
stock of Boston," she whipped out. "Take me back
at once! I will not be treated so!"

"I am tired of treating you like a lady. You need
to be handled like a stubborn female," said Jeremy grimly. "We're going somewhere and have a
quiet talk, and if that doesn't work, I'll try another
method I know to make you see things my way!"

He scared her. She shifted, as though to jump
out of the moving carriage. His hand shot out, and
he held her tightly by the arm. "You're not getting
out of this carriage until I say so!"

They were moving at a dangerously fast pace
along the cobblestoned streets, uphill and down-
hill, faster and faster. The sun beat down on
Diana's unprotected head, but she felt cold and
weak. Did he mean to carry her off—attack her?
He looked capable of anything!

She could not think clearly. Jeremy was going
on and on, one hand holding the reins, the other
gripping her arm so tightly she knew there would
be great bruises there tomorrow.

She looked about frantically. Few noted their
passing, except to call out disapprovingly that the
carriage was going too fast—who did he think he
was anyway? Seeing his uniform, they shook their
heads and muttered about sailors on leave. They
did look curiously at the lovely blonde, pale as
death, beside him in the dark carriage.

Abruptly Jeremy pulled up in front of a neat
green lawn, a yellow house with green shutters

and red brick sidewalk. He pulled up the horses, and jumped down, tying the reins to a post.

"Come along," he said, lifting his arms for her. She stared at him, and swallowed hard on her fright.

"I demand to be returned to—"

"You're coming in," he said, and yanked at her rudely. He was not polite, not gentle, not the way he had been on the ship. His eyes were still flaring green with fury.

She came. She thought he would have carried her otherwise. And she did not know where she was. It was a strange part of town. The houses were farther apart, spread out comfortably on great green lawns, with stables behind the houses. The nearest house was some distance away. Who would hear her scream? Jeremy was quite capable of clapping his hand over her mouth and forcing her with him.

She slid down with his help, and walked meekly beside him up to the strange door. Up the steps they went, but instead of knocking he flung open the carved wood door, with its neat pediment above it, and two wide windows beside it.

He drew her into the long, dark, cool hallway with him. At the first door he pushed her inside, into a large parlor much like that of Mrs. Bellows, furnished in blue and cream. The shades were drawn, and she could see only that the room was furnished with silk chairs and sofas, a fine Persian rug, a fire screen of cream and flowered embroidery.

"Sit down," said Jeremy and pushed her into a plush chair. Then he went to the door and yelled, "Mother!"

Diana started, and he came back to her, to stand scowling over her. "Mother?" she asked faintly.

"Yes, this is my home," he said. "Now, be nice to Mother, or I'll carry you off to my ship!"

He looked fiery and dangerous. Diana waited apprehensively, and finally a woman came in.

"Why, Jeremy, that was a quick visit— Oh, my dear—how do you do?" She came smilingly to Diana, who rose to greet her.

Diana saw a woman not as tall as herself, with white hair piled high and gentle blue eyes, a woman of about fifty years, with a placid, comfortable face.

"This is Lady Diana Somerville, Mother. My mother, Mrs. McCullough," growled Jeremy, as though on his quarterdeck, instructing his sailors. "The girl is mad enough to think she is going to marry that idiot!"

"Oh, dear, no, you wouldn't do that," said Bess McCullough at once. "You wouldn't, would you, dear? Jeremy has told me all about it, you see."

"She is going to marry me," said Jeremy decisively.

"Of course!" said his mother. "I have longed for you to find a sweet girl and settle down. And she does look lovely." She smiled encouragingly at Diana, who had not been able to utter a sound.

"Is that you, Jeremy? I thought I heard you yell

for Mother. What is it— Oh, hello," and in came a young lady, followed by yet another.

"The whole household; I might have expected it," groaned Jeremy. "Lady Diana Somerville, my sisters, Angela and Teresa. And I expect—yes, here comes Penelope. Where is Donald? It will only take him—"

"Donald went with your father to the office this morning, as you might have remembered if you had been paying attention at breakfast," said his mother, with a sweetly mischievous smile at him. Now Diana could see the resemblance between them; it was in their expressions.

"What's happening?" asked the youngest girl, Penelope, who appeared to be about twelve. She looked with quick curiosity at Diana, studying her gown, the ring on her hand, the diamond pendant at her throat. "Is this the lady you rescued—"

"Captured," growled Jeremy. "She is my prisoner!"

Diana gave him a bewildered look. He was striding about, watched by his three sisters with wonder, by his mother with fond amusement.

"And what is this about a marriage?" his mother said.

"Oh, you're going to marry her! Oh, wonderful!" cried the eldest sister, Angela, about Jennie's age. She clasped her hands tightly and smiled at Diana. "We have been hoping and hoping. Jeremy has been like a bear with a sore head, and we knew something was happening to him! He never paid girls much attention before, except lightly, you know."

Diana decided it was time she spoke up for herself. "I am going to marry—Sir Geoffrey Loring—on Wednesday!" she said loudly, over their voices. "The bride dress is all made—and I promised!" And she burst into tears.

At once she was drawn to the sofa and comforted by Jeremy's mother, while his sisters crowded about. "Oh, poor dear!" comforted Mrs. McCullough, patting her shoulders. "You must have been bullied into it. Jeremy said your father was cold as ice, and your fiancé worse!"

"What a marvelous accent," murmured Teresa, patting her hand. "Shall I order tea, Mother? I am sure she will want tea, she is so very English."

"Of course, dear. Bring tea, and a handkerchief. There, there, dear. It will be all right. Jeremy will take care of everything!"

Jeremy stopped pacing, and gazed down at Diana anxiously. "I don't think she has eaten for weeks, she is so thin. And her color is all gone. I know they've been bullying her. I thought I had months to court her—they promised they wouldn't let her go soon. Damn that fool, Sir Geoffrey. He would jump in—"

His mother seemed to make sense of all that, and went on patting Diana's back and making soothing sounds. Angela said, "But do tell us what happened. When you went to see her, did her father object?"

"No, he wasn't there. Sir Geoffrey was, though,

and talking about how he would marry Diana on Wednesday!" said Jeremy bitterly. "And said he would invite me to the wedding. I saw red!"

"Of course you did, dear, like any sane man," said Mrs. McCullough, nodding her white head. "And so you carried Diana away in your carriage?"

"Naturally!" Jeremy had begun to pace again, giving Diana nervous looks as she wiped her face with the handkerchief one of the girls had provided. "I had to knock him out first, though." He glanced down ruefully at his still-bloody hands.

"Angela, do get him fixed up. Take him away!" said his mother. "You know I detest to see blood. Your father will be home for luncheon in an hour or so; he shall know what to do. We must contact Lady Diana's father, and soon everything will be settled."

Despite her gentle voice, Mrs. McCullough seemed to have command of this ship, thought Diana, as Jeremy went off meekly with his sister while Teresa brought tea and sandwiches. Soon they all sat about drinking tea, and devouring Diana with their eyes.

Jeremy came back, more cheerful, his hand bandaged, and the cut on his face treated with ointment. A bruised cheekbone was turning purple, but his sisters did not seem to think it important. They were probably accustomed to his ways, Diana thought, as she sipped her tea. She managed to eat a sandwich, and felt better.

Presently his father came home. Henry McCullough was as big a man as Jeremy, and despite his white hair and wrinkles, his green eyes shone as vibrantly as his son's. He was as distinguished-looking as her father, thought Diana. Perhaps this was the way Jeremy would look when the youth and fire and wildness were burned out of him by years and experience.

Donald came in, slipping shyly past his brother to gaze at Diana and blush when he was introduced. He was a tall, thin lad. There was talk of the other two brothers, Howard at the shipyard and Anthony at his law school. What a grand big family Jeremy had, she thought wistfully. And when everyone talked at once, she felt deafened. They all had advice to offer, plans and schemes. Penelope entered the discussion as enthusiastically as the others, for all her young years.

"She must stay here with us, and we shall lock the doors and keep Sir Geoffrey away!" she said firmly. "Then he can't marry her at all!"

"But she is wearing his ring," Angela pointed out. "That means they are engaged. She must return the ring and explain to him that she can't marry him as she is going to marry Jeremy!"

Diana stared down at the diamond. Jeremy came over to her, removed the ring, and flung it in the corner. "That disposes of the ring," he proclaimed. Diana felt a little hysterical, wanting to laugh and cry all at once.

His father shook his head. "Fetch me the ring, Donald," he said sternly. Donald went over and rescued the diamond, and put it in his father's hand. The man looked at it, slipped it into his waistcoat pocket. "I shall return the ring," he said firmly. "Yes, I must call upon Lady Diana's father and explain the situation. Jeremy is too hot-tempered to do so without a battle. You really must learn to control yourself, son," he said mildly. "There is a diplomatic way of handling such things, you know."

Jeremy looked sheepish. "I wanted to kill the man," he muttered. "I thought she would be safe there for a time, but he took advantage of the situation to press for immediate marriage. He has no regard for her feelings!"

"But we must do this in a civilized manner," said Mr. McCullough. "So after luncheon I shall go and call on Lord Somerville. And also Sir Geoffrey."

"If he is conscious," muttered Jeremy.

"Conscious!" said his sisters all at once, in an excited twitter. "Oh, what have you done?" cried his mother.

"Oh, we had a bit of a dustup," said Jeremy, looking guiltily at Diana. She could not help but smile, remembering the other time he had used that phrase.

A maid came to call them for luncheon. Mrs. McCullough rose. "We will go in," she said. "Henry, pray escort Lady Diana."

Henry McCullough grinned at Diana and made her a small bow. The others went in informally, chatting and laughing. Diana was seated at Mr.

McCullough's right, with Jeremy at her right. She was sure she could eat nothing.

But the conversation was smoothly turned by Mrs. McCullough to the day's work at the shipyards, and how the new ship was progressing. Then Mr. McCullough asked her about the church choir and how the rehearsal had proceeded. And somehow Diana was able to relax, even with Jeremy close at her side, watching over her as fiercely as if he expected Sir Geoffrey to burst into the room at any moment.

She could not talk much, but she listened to them, and envied their closeness. Still she felt bewildered and lost. There was nothing much anyone could do, was there? She had promised to marry Sir Geoffrey, all the arrangements were made . . . her father was her guardian, and she did not think he would agree to her marriage to Jeremy. For how would he ever explain *that* to his superiors in London?

"We will have coffee in the drawing room and become better acquainted with Lady Diana," said Mrs. McCullough.

The woman's brisk voice interrupted Diana's thoughts, and she rose mechanically to follow the others into the drawing room. Jeremy led her to the sofa and sat down beside her, clasping her hand in his.

But Diana was beginning to recover. Jeremy might be captain of his quarterdeck, but he could not command her like one of his sailors. He had said nothing of loving her, nor of wishing to marry her, until today. He was taking too much for granted. She had not consented to anything.

She sat silent, troubled. Her father would be so angry, and she would bear the brunt of it. Her father would treat Mr. McCullough coldly and send him on his way, and nothing would be changed for Diana. She wanted to weep.

Mr. McCullough gave her a keen look and rose. "Well, I must go and call upon Lord Somerville. Lady Diana, you do wish me to return the ring to your—ah—fiancé?"

She nodded. "If he—will accept it," she said in a weary, discouraged voice. "You see, my father has arranged my marriage. That is the way it is done. I mean—we have been engaged for a year—"

"Well, well, I will see what I can do," he said kindly. "You should not be pushed into anything against your will. And, Jeremy, you are not to pester the girl! Just because she does not want to marry Sir Geoffrey does not mean she will marry you! She seemed quite confused when I came in today!"

"I love her," said Jeremy bluntly. "And if she doesn't love me yet, she soon will. At any event, we are going to be married. If I have to ask that poker of a father—"

"That will do, Jeremy," said Mrs. McCullough sternly. "You will not disparage Lady Diana's father. The girl must be free to do what she wishes."

"But you do want to marry me, don't you?" he asked, turning on Diana, squeezing her hand encouragingly.

"I—I don't know," she said, biting her lips. He had still said nothing of loving her, not to *her!*

Mrs. McCullough went to the door and motioned to her brood. "I think you had best have a frank talk with Diana," she said. "I can see that, like a man, you have taken much for granted. Talk to the girl, and see how she feels. Henry, you will return the ring for her, and give my regards to Mrs. Bellows. Lady Diana shall return to her by evening, and meantime, she shall be comfortable here. Lady Diana, if you wish anything, please ring the bell." And she nodded at the long, silken bellpull near the couch.

The McCullough family made their exit. Jeremy had stood while the ladies left. Penelope was the last to depart, and her wide, curious look told them she was reluctant to leave such a dramatic moment. Jeremy went to close the door, then returned to stand over Diana.

"Now," he began, "tell me the whole story. What made you agree so suddenly to the marriage? I thought you were settled happily with Mrs. Bellows for a few months."

Sir Geoffrey thought it would be best for us to marry," she said in a low tone. "Father said it might speed our return, that the Americans would permit a frigate to dock here and take us away."

"And you wished to hurry away from the barbaric Americans?" he said, still looming over her.

He was teasing her. She blinked back tears. He had no tender feelings for her—he was a fighter, and inclined to start a battle when he saw something taken from his grasp.

She lifted her head. "Sir, it is no concern of yours, how I feel," she said frostily. "You have caused enough trouble for today. I must ask you to return me to my father."

"And go on with that insane marriage? Diana, you are not frozen inside, I know it. When you let me kiss you on the ship—"

She jumped up. "I did not *let* you! You forced the kisses on me, sir! How dare you say I would so far forget myself—"

He put his hand boldly on her waist. "You did forget yourself," he said softly. "You yourself know it. When I held you—like this—and kissed you—like this—"

He was pulling her to him. She held back strongly, her fists pressed against his hard chest. "You have acted like a pirate!" she cried out furiously in her bewilderment and rage. "You carried me off onto the ship like a pirate! And today, just the same! Brawling and fighting and knocking out poor Sir Geoffrey—"

"A pirate? I feel like a pirate with you. I would carry you off with me to a desert island, and make love to you night and day—"

He yanked her to him, caught her off balance, and pulled her right against him. She felt the warmth of his body against her thin muslin dress, the steel hardness of his arm about her waist, his other hand in her tumbled hair as he held her face up to his. His mouth came down on hers, and the ruthless, passionate kisses burned her throat, her mouth. Her breath caught, she could not move or speak, crushed there against him.

"Diana, Diana," he whispered at last, holding her off a little to gaze into her dazed blue eyes. "I have dreamed of you like this, close to me. I went a little crazy when you said you were going to marry that idiot. You will marry me soon—"

"No," she said weakly. "You ignored me for weeks, you scarcely thought of me—"

"My sweet! I thought of nothing but you! But how quickly could I move? I meant to woo you slowly and gently, call on you at times, make you think of me. Then I would approach your father, beg his permission to consider me as a son-in-law. Cut out that idiot with his scarlet coat and his snuffbox. You couldn't marry such a clod, could you, Diana?"

"We are going to be married on Wednesday," she managed feebly. "It is—all arranged— Oh, Jeremy!"

For his mouth came down on the pulse beat of her throat, and she was lost in the sweet storm of his embrace. He moved his lips over her throat, to her shoulder, pushed aside the soft fabric to press his mouth there fiercely.

"You'll marry naught but me," he whispered in her ear, kissing it until she was dizzy with his caresses. "Diana, Diana, you love me, you must love me—"

"I do—love you," she finally whispered. "I never thought it was possible for me to love anyone in the world. I was always so alone. I felt cold inside. You see—my father was cold to me, and Mother was kept from me by his demands. I grew up concealing my feelings until I finally thought I could feel nothing for anyone."

He listened thoughtfully, tenderly, as she told him of the lonely years. "But that is all over, my darling girl. You shall have my family for yours. You shall not be alone again, for I shall be with you."

She thought of something else. "But—your ship, Jeremy. You will go off—"

"No," he said gently. "Not if I marry. Father wishes me to come into the business with him. There is much more to do than before. I can help design the ships, see them to completion. There are others who can captain the ships and go off to fight. A man with a family must put the family first, my precious, and so you shall ever be to me. First in my heart and my life."

"You will miss the sea," she said feebly, but her eyes gave her away, blazing with happiness.

"The sea is always here. And when peace comes, we can sail off down the coast, and off to adventure together. There are islands you must see, beautiful ones with white sand and dark palms, and moonlight on flowers such as you have never seen. Oh, Diana— I want to show you the beauties of the world, the loveliness of it—"

Somehow they were on the couch together, clinging closely. Her arms had found their way around his neck. He kissed her slowly, possessively, then drew back. His hand moved over the muslin of her back, back to her shoulders. His touch was fiery to her.

"Diana," he said seriously, his green eyes intent. "I wish to marry you. I have loved you since I first looked up in that Russian's study and saw a vision of loveliness gazing at me with cool blue eyes. Not frightened, not screaming, just looking at me. I could scarcely think. I wanted to carry you off at once. And I in the middle of stealing important papers."

"Oh, Jeremy!" Her arms clasped closer about his neck. She dared to caress his hair, and bring a glint to his green eyes. "You were so brazen, so bold! I had never met anyone like you. Yet I was not frightened—somehow I did not think you would harm me."

"Never, never, my precious!" He bent his head to kiss her again slowly, sweetly, a long, lingering kiss that sent blood to her head and made her wildly dizzy. He was shaking a little when he let her draw back from him. "God, I shall have to marry you soon, Diana. I can scarce keep control over myself! I want you so madly. And you love me also, do you not?" His cheek caressed hers; she loved the rough masculine feel of it against her own.

All the coldness was gone as she responded to the possession and love in his voice. They held each other, whispering how they had first come to love. Her face was wildly flushed now, all paleness gone. He ruffled up her hair, then smoothed it down, told her how he loved her, how he had ached to be with her that first week.

"But I thought you would be all right with Mrs. Bellows. She's a good sort, sensible. That damned Sir Geoffrey—" he growled.

She delighted in smoothing out the lines of his face with her fingers, and he caught her hand and kissed the tips of each finger in turn.

The door opened cautiously, a head came in. "It's all right, Mother, they're kissing!" cried Penelope.

"Penelope, you come here this minute!" cried Angela.

The door slammed. Diana pulled away in great embarrassment. "Those damn girls!" laughed Jeremy. "You see how it is, Diana, with a family! Too curious by half! Well, I suppose we had best tell Mother and the girls. What about a week from now?"

"For what?" asked Diana, trying to smooth her hair with one hand while he held the other.

"For our wedding, of course! You don't think I intend to wait, do you? You said the bride dress was ready!"

"Oh, Jeremy," she said weakly, and he kissed her again.

But she would consent to nothing until she had heard from her father. She never knew what Mr. McCullough said to him. Lord Somerville was reticent on that point, and her new father-in-law was bland. However, Dora whispered to her later that they had had a vast argument in the drawing room, and talked for nigh on three hours! She had crept close to the windows from the garden until her mother had called her away, and she had heard Lord Somerville cursing!

However, Lord Somerville was reconciled in some manner to the match. Mr. McCullough was a man of substance in Boston, owning his own shipyards. Jeremy was part owner, and he planned to build a home of his own for himself and Diana. And when Lord Somerville saw Diana that evening, radiant, her hand clasped tightly in Jeremy's, he could not refuse her.

The ring was returned to Sir Geoffrey. He sailed for home the following week on a British frigate that was miraculously given permission to land for just that purpose. He sailed alone, taking his diamond tiara with him, and a load of tobacco to sell in the home country.

Lord Somerville remained to give his daughter away. On her wedding morning, as she came down in the beautiful white gown and veil, he told her, "You have never looked so much like your mother, my dear."

"Thank you, Father. You—you have been very good to me—and Jeremy." She clasped his hands. He seemed a little warmer today, and rather lonely, gazing at her with a faint wistfulness.

"Nonsense. Couldn't do anything else but give you your mother's jewels, and a proper trousseau. And Jeremy should have the money toward his house. You should have a decent home. Well, well,

I'll try to come back and visit you. Your brother shall come also, once this damned war is over."

"I pray it will be soon, Father. I am sure you will do all in your considerable power to bring that about. You will speak to the Prince Regent about it, will you not?"

"You know I will." He cleared his voice impatiently. Something about Diana's fragile beauty today caught at his heart. "Can't have our countries at odds. Well, you have a beautiful day for your wedding."

The girls were waiting for her in their beautiful gowns. Amy had asked Diana dolefully if she no longer wanted her and her sisters, now that she was not going to marry Sir Geoffrey. "Of course I do," Diana had said. "I shall have a big, big wedding, with all you girls, and Jeremy's sisters and brothers."

It was one of the most splendid weddings Boston had ever seen, that beautiful late August day. Diana went in on her father's arm. He was distinguished in gray silk with rubies at his wrists and on his white stock. Angela walked in with Jennie, Teresa with her friend Amy, and Penelope with Dora.

Jeremy was waiting at the altar with his three brothers, Howard, Anthony, and young Donald. All Diana saw was Jeremy—in his blue uniform, white knee breeches, with gold on his shoulders, just as she had seen him on the deck of his Yankee brig.

Her pirate, she thought, smiling at him from behind the sheer lace veil.

At the reception later, Diana recognized many of her new friends, plus the officials who had interviewed her when she arrived in Boston. And there was the first mate, Eli Ulrich, with his wife, and several of their children. Eli beamed as though he had personally planned it all himself.

The other men from the ship had come, even Captain Talbot, who could have returned to England with Sir Geoffrey. But he had remained for the wedding, he told Diana. "Couldn't miss it, Lady Diana!"

"Mrs. McCullough," Jeremy corrected him gaily.

"I must be careful how I handle my ship from now on," he told them ruefully, bending over to whisper. "Can't always lose such treasure as I did this voyage!"

Jeremy grinned at her. "Best engagement I ever fought," he said, a twinkle in his green eyes. They all laughed.

Diana was led to a huge, many-tiered white cake. Jeremy lent her his dress sword and helped her cut the first piece, his white-gloved hand over hers. Then she could step back, sip her champagne, and beam at the girls who crowded about her. Her own new family, she thought. How dear they were!

Bess McCullough had kissed her and blessed her like a daughter. Angela had promised to help Diana in her adjustment to the new life, telling her of American customs. She was a serious-minded girl, already looking forward to her own wedding this winter.

Diana and Jeremy would live first in a wing of the McCullough house. But Jeremy had impatiently started the building of a new house not far from that of his parents, on a tract of land he already owned. It had five acres of grassland, some fruit trees, and a small stream. He and Diana had pored over drawings, made plans for the drawing room, bedrooms, kitchen, a terrace, brick walks, a captain's walk on the roof. It would be a typical Boston home, nothing grand like the London town house, but a real home, she thought, in a daze of delight.

After the wedding, the carriage was brought around. Their trunks were already strapped on the back. With many calls of good wishes, and some tossing of silver-papered roses and horseshoes, they were off.

They would drive the rest of the day, arriving in late evening at a friend's summer cottage on the ocean. There they would walk on the beach, gaze out to the sea, talk, or be silent. To be alone for the first time ever.

Jeremy was quiet for a time as he drove out of the Boston traffic, until they came to the countryside north of the city. Then he leaned back with a sigh of relief.

"Whew, that's over," he said. "Feel better, Diana?"

"Much better," she said demurely. "It *has* been hot today, hasn't it?"

He gave her a long, slow look. She had changed from her white wedding dress into a simple blue muslin.

"I like that dress," he said.

She smiled and tucked her hand in his arm rather shyly. It had all been so sudden, she could not believe they really belonged to each other. "I like your family so much," she said dreamily. "I think I have always longed to be part of a big family. They make me feel so welcome."

"You like large families, and so do I," said Jeremy. He gave her a mischievous look. "We must see to it that we have a large family, Diana. Then you shall never feel lonely again!"

"Oh, Jeremy," she said, growing pink. He laughed aloud, and a farmer returning from the fields gave them a curious look, then a friendly wave, which they returned.

"I'll take you home to England sometime," he said, more seriously. "You will want to see your father and brother again. And I'll see to it that they come here. You don't want to lose touch with them. However, you know that my family is yours now. They love you already."

She leaned against his shoulder, watching dreamily as the sun cast longer and longer shadows across the green and golden fields. It was a different land, but it was her land now, her America. "Oh, Jeremy, I never thought, that night at the ball, when I first met you—"

"And little did I think I had met my fate! I only knew I wanted to see you again, and again. I cursed that I had to return to my ship so soon. And then—"

And they began to exchange sweet reminiscences about days and nights on the ship. The carriage rolled on across the countryside, and the sun cast a red glow over the ocean waves and the creamy sands.

It was dark when they reached the cottage. Jeremy jumped down, tied the horses firmly, then came around to reach up for Diana. She slipped down into his arms, and he closed them tightly about her.

As he kissed her, she could hear the waves of the ocean beating against the sandy shores—the same ocean that had seemed so wide and fearful when she had first set out. But it had brought her love to her. And she would never be lonely and afraid again.

*A tempestuous love that blazes
across continents and burns beyond desire . . .
beyond forgetting . . .*

LOVE'S WILDEST FIRES

by Christina Savage

A woman rages against the boundless passion that
enslaves her to a man she has sworn to hate. He won her
hand in a game of cards . . . but lost her heart when
a shattering secret revealed on their wedding night
turned tender new love into terrible fury.
LOVE'S WILDEST FIRES is a timeless saga about a
man possessed by the splendorous wild land and the
woman whose heart was wilder still.

A DELL BOOK $1.95

Something peculiar is happening in
Port Arbello.
The children are disappearing,
one by one.

Suffer the Children

A Novel by John Saul

An evil history that occurred one hundred years ago
is repeating itself.

Only one man heard a pretty little girl begin to
scream. He watched her struggle and die, then stilled
his guilty heart by dashing himself to death in the
sea . . .

Now that strange, terrified child has ended her silence
with the scream that began a century ago. Don't miss
this tale of unnatural passion and supernatural terror!

A Dell Book $1.95

Dell Bestsellers

- [ ] **BLOOD AND MONEY** by Thomas Thompson . **$2.50** (10679-6)
- [ ] **THE DOCTOR'S WIFE** by Brian Moore **$2.25** (11931-6)
- [ ] **MAGIC** by William Goldman **$1.95** (15141-4)
- [ ] **THE USERS** by Joyce Haber **$2.25** (19264-1)
- [ ] **THE OTHER SIDE OF MIDNIGHT**
  by Sidney Sheldon **$1.95** (16067-7)
- [ ] **EYES** by Felice Picano **$1.95** (12427-1)
- [ ] **THE HITE REPORT** by Shere Hite **$2.75** (13690-3)
- [ ] **SURGEON UNDER THE KNIFE**
  by William A. Nolen, M.D. **$1.95** (18388-X)
- [ ] **BEULAH LAND** by Lonnie Coleman **$2.25** (11393-8)
- [ ] **THE GEMINI CONTENDERS** by Robert Ludlum **$2.25** (12859-5)
- [ ] **GRAHAM: A DAY IN BILLY'S LIFE**
  by Gerald S. Strober **$1.95** (12870-6)
- [ ] **LOVE'S WILDEST FIRES** by Christina Savage . **$1.95** (12895-1)
- [ ] **SUFFER THE CHILDREN** by John Saul **$1.95** (18293-X)
- [ ] **SLIDE** by Gerald A. Browne **$1.95** (17701-4)
- [ ] **ACAPULCO** by Burt Hirschfeld **$1.95** (10402-5)
- [ ] **RICH FRIENDS** by Jacqueline Briskin **$1.95** (17380-9)
- [ ] **THE LONG DARK NIGHT** by Joseph Hayes . **$1.95** (14824-3)
- [ ] **MARATHON MAN** by William Goldman ... **$1.95** (15502-9)
- [ ] **IT CHANGED MY LIFE** by Betty Friedan ... **$2.25** (13936-8)
- [ ] **THE CHOIRBOYS** by Joseph Wambaugh ... **$2.25** (11188-9)

At your local bookstore or use this handy coupon for ordering:

DELL BOOKS
P.O. BOX 1000, PINEBROOK, N.J. 07058

Please send me the books I have checked above. I am enclosing $_____
(please add 35¢ per copy to cover postage and handling). Send check or money
order—no cash or C.O.D.'s. Please allow up to 8 weeks for shipment.

Mr/Mrs/Miss_____

Address_____

City_____ State/Zip_____
